LITTLE MISS KICK-ASS

My Destiny
By Felicity Kates

Copyright

LITTLE MISS KICK-ASS
My Destiny

is a reissue of
FIT TO BE TIED
By Felicity Kates

First edition. July 31, 2015
Reissued Feb 2016
Copyright © 2015 and 2016 Felicity Kates

Written by Felicity Kates.
Edited by Piper Denna.
Cover art and design by Kate Reed.

© Egorr | Dreamstime.com - Nude Sensual Couple Photo

Dedication

To all of my little ones dancing in the sky with the stars.
Mamma will always love you.
xx

Acknowledgements

To Shannon and all my reading friends at the <u>Kates Korner Fan Page</u>—thank you! Without you and your love of reading, this book would never have reached 'The End.'

To Zara, writing goddess and inspiration, Piper, editor extraordinaire, and Treena, my P.A., without whom I would be a disorganized mess.

To Tammy and the Rockstars, and my white knight, Lucian. Thank you from the bottom of my heart. I couldn't do this without you, my friends.

To my husband, Mike, my son, Alex and all my wonderful friends and family cheering me on behind the scenes. I would be lost without each of you and your belief in me. Thank you.

To S.K. for your help with Swedish translation. Thank you for helping me get the wording just right.

And to R.B. whom I met by chance many years ago while on vacation in London, but whose Swedish accent and warm blue eyes have never been forgotten.

Thank you so much to all of you!

~Felicity~

Table of Contents

Chapter 1

It could be a dream.

I'm flying, slipping through white clouds into the brilliant blue sky. Golden sunlight arcs off of snow-swept fields and crowns the distant mountains. And there's the lake, a dazzling frozen jewel set in the icy landscape below.

At thirty thousand feet in the air, the familiar beauty spread out beneath me never ceases to take my breath away. Nestled amongst the snow and trees, rooftops huddle together along white lines of freshly driven roads. Kiruna: the northernmost city in Sweden, an oasis sculpted from ice and pine.

It could be a dream. But the vivid reality of coming home after almost ten years jars my thoughts like a heart-racing nightmare. The kind that jerks me awake at night, forcing me to face the dark emptiness of my life.

Why have I come back to this place of cold memory? This land where my life began and where it went to hell.

"Excuse me, Mr. Lindstrom, but we'll be starting our descent soon. The Captain is requesting that everyone fasten their seatbelts."

"Thank you, Lisa."

The tall, leggy and raven-haired flight attendant's appreciative smile holds every ounce of promise I expect. But despite the fact that she's been more than adequate as a crew member on my private jet, and as an occasional lover in my bed, I don't return her interest.

For the last four weeks, there hasn't been a cell in my body remotely attracted to her, or any other person in this gods-forsaken universe, except one.

Astrid Bitten.

The lithe blonde sitting across from me in the cabin's spacious seating, doing her best to pretend I don't exist—and failing amusingly in the attempt.

"Can I get you anything else, sir?"

I return Lisa's lingering look with a curt shake of my head. "No."

A small frown touches her brow as her gaze flashes to Astrid. "Anything for you, Miss?"

Astrid's full lips pull into a polite smile. "No, thank you."

Lisa snatches up my empty glass of Evian and Astrid's barely-touched glass of white wine, and moves off down the cabin, pausing briefly to check on the rest of my guests. But I really don't care who she talks to or what she does. My focus is pinned on Astrid's slender fingers as she nervously fumbles with the connection on her seatbelt.

Even though I know she'll refuse out of principle, I can't resist asking, "Need some help?" as I snap my own latch into place.

"No," she mutters.

"Suit yourself, my goddess."

"Don't fucking call me that," she mutters as my endearment strikes a nerve.

"Why not? It's true." She is a goddess. My goddess, whether she wants to believe it or not.

"No, it's not. It's asinine. Like you." Her frown twists into a smug—if somewhat relieved—smile of victory as a sharp click signals her success with the belt buckle.

"Keep it coming, gorgeous," I say with a wink. "You know how much your wicked mouth turns me on."

"Fu—" she starts to snarl, then stops when she glances down at the obvious hard-on bulging my chinos. With a strained smile she changes tactics and bats her baby blues at me in mock innocence. "Whatever you say, Mr. Lindstrom."

Her simpering tone makes my grin widen.

She hates me for the man I am, the control I have. The awakening I've caused within her—though I suspect she does not yet realize that it is the root of her anger.

We sit on this plane, sipping drinks and watching the world move beneath us, cloaked in a veneer of normalcy that couldn't be further from the truth.

With the whisper of a word and a concentrated thought, I can bend that truth, twist it and make it mine. If I'm willing to accept the cost. Normality is a fragile comfort. I've never known anyone to give up the illusion without a fight.

I've lived my own life safely under a guise of ordinariness for so long I can almost believe the lie. Perhaps that was why, four weeks ago, I thought it would be a fun joke to attend the Fanglorious Fan Expo convention in Chicago dressed as a superhero instead of cloaked in my usual businessman attire.

It was amusing to walk amongst throngs of comic book fans parading around in costumes. Completely ironic to be in a place where superhuman qualities were celebrated, and yet utterly misunderstood. But even more extraordinary was meeting Astrid Bitten.

So unexpected to have felt that tingle of recognition pulling at my insides.

She was sitting at the *Steam Bunny* booth, helping to sell a graphic novel about a woman with superpowers, while completely clueless about her own mystical gifts. She chatted awkwardly with the fans waiting in line for autographs, her back straight and blond hair pulled into a ponytail, and sporting the sexiest pair of legs I've ever seen. My cock swelled so hard so fast, I had to have her.

Was it selfishness that caused me to fuck her senseless that afternoon and awaken her true nature?

Undoubtedly.

I won't argue that her anger and mistrust toward me aren't justified, but after nearly thirty days of her constant rebuttal to the obvious fact that she and I belong together, my patience is wearing thin.

My cock is a hard throb, my hunger to ravish her a gnawing pain that bites my soul. Sitting this close without touching her is like a torturous rasp across my skin. I can smell her honey-warm scent in the air. The only thing that makes the agony of waiting bearable is the certainty that I will fuck her senseless again very soon.

There is no other option for her and me.

Not when I'm so aroused each breath is a tight ache. Not when I'm returning to the place of my birth, this place of raw power. As soon as we step off the plane, Astrid will begin to feel it too. The primal energy resonating from our ancient northern ancestry will call to her in the alpine climate, heating her blood as it does mine.

Our mating under the stars is as inevitable as the sunrise.

Our inherent natures demand it, even if the gods do not.

I shift in my seat, a slight readjustment as the inevitable guilt-filled memories rattle against the mental door I've locked them behind. What price will the gods extract from me this time for desiring the life of an ordinary man?

I have been careful, very careful, to keep the choice hers, to learn from the lesson they taught me and not repeat the mistakes of my past.

But as I sit here and watch her struggle with the attraction she feels for me, I know there isn't anything in the world I will not give for the chance to live the rest of my life with this woman. I'll even face the inescapable pain that returning home brings.

As the heated silence between us builds, she turns to stare out the window, but not before I catch her haughty glare: a flash of blue fire, rimmed with golden lashes. Crimson lips. Creamy cheeks. A face I crave kissing with her generous mouth and the saucy way she likes to use it. And gods above, her skin. So smooth and unblemished, just like the rest of her. No tats or piercings, not even an earring hangs from her cute little lobes. Just the tiniest of birthmarks, right in the crease behind her left ear, marking her as the extraordinary woman I know her to be, even if she's not yet ready to accept it.

Perhaps sensing my stare, she tucks a strand of silky hair around the shell of her ear and sweeps the length over her shoulder, exposing the steady pulse fluttering at her neck.

I've made that pulse race. Not just once or twice, over a dozen times during that weekend we met. Enjoyed the hot flush, which spreads between her beautiful breasts and up her slender neck as she comes. I made her scream in pleasure every time she orgasmed, her whole body quivering as I filled her with my seed. No artifice. No pretense. No startled questions of, "What the hell was that?" when a little zing of energy escaped my control and was released. Just pure, honest ecstasy. She took all I had and then wanted more.

She's strong, fiery and beautiful.

A lethal combination for my sanity.

How else can I explain the lengths I've undertaken to not use my powers of influence, giving her time to see the obvious on her own instead?

She left me tied up in a hotel room, for Christ's sake, ass-naked except for a ridiculous superhero mask. I could have made her fuck me six ways to Sunday for that, in front of a million people, if I chose.

And here she is, trying so damned hard to pretend I don't exist.

I can't help laughing. Not that I care if she sees me enjoying the show she's putting on. She's made a point of not looking at me since boarding the flight, in between sneaking peeks so full of heat that my dick is hard enough to pierce steel.

The fact that I could have her on her knees in an instant, begging for my cock, is just one more torment in the irony of our situation. I can feel the energy building inside me. One word, one focused thought and the molecules vibrating in the air between us will carry my desire to her, alter her perception, and make my will her own.

And, merciful gods, she does know how to suck my cock with an expertise I've been unable to forget since that evening we met. Hell, even without her luscious lips and fit, slender body, her very name arouses me in a way I've not experienced in, well…ever.

Astrid: *beautiful as a goddess.*

Her parents couldn't have named her better. Did they know the tiny birthmark behind her ear marked her as a descendant of *Sarahkka,* a Sami fertility goddess?

My goddess. My destiny.

A truth I need to deal with before this insane obsession with her completely derails my carefully organized life.

I've found myself doing things over the past several weeks, things I never considered before Astrid became entangled in my existence. Stupid things, like orchestrating this agonizingly awkward trip to Sweden when every instinct screams for me to avoid the nightmare and stay in L.A.

I could do business via the web just as easily. Unless, of course, that business is Astrid Bitten. Taming her the non-superpower way, I've discovered to my annoyance, requires more than a quick text. Not that texting doesn't have its uses.

Removing my phone from the charger molded into my seat, I type a short message:

This weekend your ass is mine, Amazon Woman.

She jerks as her phone chimes in her vest pocket. When she glances at the screen, her mouth twitches at the sizzling reminder of the dress-up game we played the weekend we first met.

Her fingers tap a reply on her phone as a smirk pulls at her lips.

In your dreams, Bat-dick.

"Bat-dick?"

Her gaze drops to my crotch and studies the contours of my tailored chinos in a sweep of raw need that licks at my insides. "Bat-dick," she asserts, her raised brow challenging me to deny her claim.

Goddammit! My fingers curl around my phone as the energy inside me screams to be released. I want to make her do more than just look. But I force myself to relax and exert restraint over my desire. I made a vow to never use my power and influence her, promised that her choices will always be her own. And even if she does not yet comprehend the cost of that pledge, I will stand by it. I will not lose this chance at redemption.

"Have you forgotten what my cock looks like, sweetheart?" I tease, flirting with the danger of losing control as much as with her. "Do I need to remind you?"

Stretching my legs out, I capture the seriously fuckable length of her shapely legs between mine, and grasp the zipper on my fly. I've been staring at her black leggings for hours, memorizing the curve of her slender calves and the contour of her thighs, itching to mouth-fuck the shadowy gap where her legs disappear beneath her black skirt. Her pussy tastes beyond divine, and I can smell how deliciously aroused she is, sitting across from me in that leather chair.

"Stop that," she hisses as if knowing exactly where my thoughts reside.

Her booted feet jerk away from me as she tucks them beneath her seat and tugs her short skirt closer to her knees. But she seems unable to move her gaze from the bulge swelling beneath my fly as I lazily play with my zipper.

"Why?" I rub my palm along the length of my cock where it throbs against my chinos, pleasure and pain ricocheting through my groin at the touch.

That beautiful blush I've craved for weeks spreads like a hot lick up her neck and stains her cheeks. Her eyes edge upward from my groin and dart toward the seats close behind her in the elegant interior of my jet.

"Because a camera crew is sitting right over there," she says in a low, insistent tone. "Not to mention Casey and Lucas."

Such misplaced modesty. "I doubt they will care. They seem, rather, ah...occupied."

The strawberry-blond beauty and her dark-haired fiancé are more interested in each other than the fact they are in company. Casey is busy exploring Lucas's ear with nibbles and kisses, while his hands are engaged in discovering the parts of her curvy body hidden beneath her sweater.

The three-member film crew, hired for the TV show, isn't bothering to pretend not to notice the action going on, and the happy couple couldn't care less. But that, of course, is the reason I've pursued them for my current business venture.

As investments go, Casey Jackson and Lucas Haskell are talented and dynamic and I expect my decision to turn their graphic novel series, *Steam Bunny*, into an animated franchise is a sound one. Even if the opportunistic marketing ploy to showcase their upcoming wedding as a reality TV show is precipitated by other, more carnal, factors.

In the realm of TV production, either the Haskells' brand of personal magnetism is destined to be ratings gold, or my instincts are out of line. And when it comes to business, my instincts are never out of line. Unfortunately, I can't say the same for my love life.

I rub my hand over the swelling bulge in my pants, drawing Astrid's hot stare down to my crotch again. "Don't be shy," I tease. "I know how much you want it." Five minutes alone in my hotel room at the convention, and she begged to peel off my ridiculous Bat Guy costume and see first-hand that I don't need padding to give me muscle. Anywhere.

"That was before I knew what you are."

"Really?" Although she may have certain suspicions, I'm certain she hasn't yet grasped that truth. "What exactly do you think I am, Astrid?"

"A liar. A selfish bastard. A cheat." She counts off my sins on her fingers. "Do I need to go on?"

Ah, no. I can't deny that I've been those things and more at various times in my life. I've never disowned that fact. But at least she's finally talking to me about it in more than one-word sentences comprised of 'fuck-you'.

The blue-balled ache in my crotch rocket will have to wait a bit longer for attention. I abandon my fly and slide my palms down my thighs as I bend forward. Resting my elbows on my knees, I wait for her gaze to find mine.

When it does, her eyes spark with the hurt and mistrust burning within her.

"I never lied to you," I say with as much conviction as I can put into my voice without resorting to using my unique gift in persuasion. If she's going to trust me, she needs to do so on her own.

"No? So sleeping with me to get a deal with my best friend was what? Honest business?" Her eyes flash with anger as she speaks in hushed tones. "You used me, Race. Just like you're using me now for this stupid reality TV show. If I didn't love Casey and Lucas so much, there's no way in hell I'd ever be here as part of this wedding crap. So just shove it with your games and your lies."

Crossing her arms over her chest, she settles back against her seat and resumes looking out her window.

So edgy and untrusting. Not that I can blame her, but damn. How can I explain to her any differently than the few hundred times I've already tried? What will it take to get her to understand, without using my gods-given gift of influence, that meeting her at that Fan Expo convention changed my life forever?

Yes, I went there for business. Yes, my intention was to swindle a deal. And, yes, I set out to do so by compromising the fiery relationship between Lucas and Casey. But it wasn't the Buxom Bunny who caught my eye.

Maybe I should have ignored my attraction for Astrid and kept on walking by. Saved us from the pain we're experiencing now by keeping everything strictly business. But being around her eased the lonely ache, even as it twisted it with memories best left buried. And I couldn't deny the startling realization, which imprinted on my body that first intensely erotic night we shared, that maybe, just maybe, the gods have handed me a precious second chance.

I'll be damned before I'll let that go, no matter how stubborn she is.

"I fell in love with you." It's the honest truth, but the mistake in saying so is obvious the moment the words blurt from my mouth.

"Oh, please," she scoffs as she stiffens in her chair, clearly offended by the idea. "Don't even start with that bullshit. That's low, even for you."

"It's not bullshit."

"No?" She presses her fingers to her temples and sucks in a breath, fighting for calm. "Do you even know what love is, Race?" she asks, her patronizing tone loaded with anger as she folds her hands in her lap.

"Yes."

I've felt the pleasure of it burn in my chest, seeming so long ago now, at Charity's first shy kiss. And I've felt the absolute agony of it as the body of my wife grew cold in my arms. The rage and helplessness of knowing, that even with all the unique power I was born with, there was nothing I could do to stop death.

Yes, I have loved. And I vowed never to fall victim to the gut-wrenching insanity again. Yet here I am, more insane than ever, at the mercy of Astrid's rejection.

White knuckled, her hands grip the armrests as the plane banks toward Kiruna. Out of the corner of my eye, the small city looms large in the window, but if Astrid notices the dazzling view, it doesn't show. Her nostrils flare, her gaze fixed squarely on me.

"We fucked, Race. You got what you wanted. I learned my lesson. End of story. So stop trying to prove what a con you are. I get it."

No, she didn't get it. Not by a long shot.

"Just tell me one thing," I say and wait for her to stop rolling her eyes and settle her gaze on mine again. "Before you knew my name. When you thought I was just some guy in a costume. How did it feel when we were together?"

Exciting. Beautiful. Alive.

I see the truths we both experienced flash within her eyes before her expression turns hot with shame. She sucks in a breath and blinks, her chin lifting slightly. Wary. Distrustful.

She opened for me so briefly, but the beauty I saw within her stole my heart. My crumpled, damaged heart. Does she think I enjoy feeling this vulnerability? This painful re-awakening?

"It was fun. That was all," she snaps.

"That wasn't all." Not even remotely. One day soon I'll have to explain the full extent of my secrets to her as I'm certain she must already have questions about her own. But first, she needs to trust me. "Now who's lying, Astrid?" I can't help prodding.

She felt the recognition in her soul. I saw it in her eyes and smile when she looked at me the moment we met at the convention. I saw it in her dreams while she slept beside me that one precious night we shared.

Before the so-called truth of my narcissistic business identity intruded, and the callous shell I worked so hard to build out of my loss and pain came back to bite me. Hard.

Race Lindstrom: professional asshole and womanizer.

The betrayal I knew she would feel as soon as she recognized my name took root with swift, uncompromising fury. She clings to it now as a shield. But it's a shield I fully intend to crack. Swiftly. And without mercy.

Whether she wants to accept it or not, she is mine.

"Do me a favor, Race? Don't talk to me for the rest of this trip. Don't look at me. Don't touch me. Just leave me the hell alone."

"I can't. You were right about one thing, Astrid." I lick my lips as her own purse in frustration. "I am a selfish bastard. I love you. I want you. And I won't stop until you are moaning my name with my cock buried deep inside you. Bliss, sweetheart. I'm going to give you fucking bliss, or die trying."

Chapter 2
ASTRID

"This…is utter bullshit," I announce as I enter my room at the Ice Hotel.

Startled by my angry tone, the porter helping with my bags darts me a mortified glance as he drops my carryon onto the hard-packed snow flooring with a muffled thud.

"Are you kidding me? It's beautiful!" Casey says with a grin as she twirls about the brightly lit room, taking in the decor. "An ice fantasy. Same as my room, except mine is a Magical Moon and Stars theme. But I like this Northern Lights room, too. You'll have to excuse my friend," she adds for the porter, whose dark brows arch high as he unloads the rest of my bags more gently. "She doesn't get out much, and just between you and me," she steps closer to his side and lowers her voice conspiratorially, "I think she was born swearing."

"Like you should talk, Ms. Pottymouth," I say, recovering my wits as I survey the bedroom suite.

It really is quite beautiful, just like the rest of the hotel. Each room is set up like an art exhibit as much as a place to sleep, and this one is no different. Everything—the walls, floor, ceiling and even the chairs—is carved from ice and snow and sculpted to perfection.

Translucent ice night tables bracket a cozy, duvet-covered, double bed with an ornately carved antler headboard, also made of clear ice. A wintery forest scene has been sculpted into the walls, with pine tree branches sweeping upwards, intersecting with deer antler patterns. Accent lighting flickers behind the trees, arcing across the white ceiling in waves of blue and green light. Radiant ice orbs have been placed about the room, lighting up the sculpted serenity like stars. Their soft brilliance glitters as the glow splashes across the gleaming surfaces of clear, polished ice. The effect is quite breathtaking, and I can't help but feel awed at the craftsmanship involved in creating something so beautiful out of frozen water.

But the faint, yet unmistakable scent of Race Lindstrom permeates the room with an earthy manliness unique to him that always reminds me of an alpine forest. I'd know it anywhere. The memory of it has haunted my dreams for the last four weeks. Not to mention his bags are sitting on the floor by the bed with their little golden 'RL' monograms quite visible against the black leather.

I attempt an apologetic smile for the porter's sake. "I'm really very sorry, but I think there's been a mistake. This appears to be Mr. Lindstrom's room."

"No mistake, Ms. Bitten," he says in Swedish-accented English. "This is one of our premium rooms designed for your comfort. Complete with pillow top mattress, deer skin rugs, and a fully heated washroom through the doorway to your left. Mr. Lindstrom did not explain this to you when he made the arrangements?"

"Race set this up?" Well, what did I expect? If he didn't let me sit alone on the plane ride, of course he'd never let me sleep in my own room at the hotel. But after the games he's played, I'll be damned if I'll be staying anywhere with him.

"Yes. He's taken care of everything for you and your friends. We are very happy and honored you've chosen the Ice Hotel for filming your upcoming wedding." He smiles at Casey then glances back at me. "Is there anything I can get for you, to make your stay more pleasant?"

"Sure. You can find me another room, please."

His expression turns uncomfortable. He's young, maybe in his early twenties, and clearly not used to being in this kind of awkward situation. "I'm afraid the Ice Hotel is very popular this weekend. I will, of course, check to be certain, but with the end-of-season tourists and the excitement about Mr. Lindstrom and your show, I believe all the rooms are full."

"Of course they are." I try to bite back my rising frustration, but I'm certain it must still show.

The excitement about Mr. Lindstrom.

The words jangle my already shredded nerves, making me seethe inside. So much for the theory that this trip was supposed to be low-key, a quick weekend jaunt to get preliminary location footage for the stupid wedding show.

Like a rock star chased by groupies, Race was mobbed by a crowd of people at the airport, including some sickeningly gorgeous women whose enthusiastic hugs and kisses made it very clear they were more than ready to welcome him home in every sense of the term.

And what did the idiot do?

He went off with the crowd, tossing a wink in my direction, and abandoned the rest of us during the relatively short journey from Kiruna's airport to the nearby town of Jukkasjarvi, home of the world famous Ice Hotel.

I shouldn't be surprised. The guy is notorious for shagging loose women the world over.

I should be glad to be away from him, but his absence—and my suspicions as to how he's occupying the time apart—hasn't done anything other than make me want to kick his ass all the way to freakin' hell.

With a mental shrug, I give up on trying to keep my irritation inside. "Well, then," I snap at the porter. "I'll take this room, and you can take Mr. Lindstrom's bags outside. He can sleep in the snow for all I care. Because I sure as hell am not sleeping with him *ever again*." And grasping Race's suitcases, I drag them toward the door.

Lying dickhead. Telling me he loves me.

I was such an idiot to sleep with Race at that convention. I *knew* better than to trust him. Knew to keep it casual and not let him get close. Knew he'd hurt me if I did. Hadn't he even warned me that he'd break my heart?

But I've never been good at casual, and sure enough I picked the worst guy possible for a one-night stand. Race is stunningly gorgeous, no doubt about it. He's built like a Viking sex-god incarnate. But he's also arrogant, selfish, and for reasons I'd rather not contemplate, hell bent on not letting our so-called relationship die.

As I drag Race's bags out the door and into the hallway, the porter scrambles to assist me, saying, "Ms. Bitten, I don't think Mr. Lindstrom will be pleased."

"Good." I hand him a few *kronor* from my pocket and am slightly mollified with how his eyes grow wide when he glances at the amount. Yeah, Race isn't the only person who can throw some weight around with money. "Thanks for your help," I say and shut the door on his astonished face, the panes of frosted glass rattling slightly with the force of my annoyance.

"Well," Casey says into the ensuing silence, green eyes narrowing on me with a knowing smile. "Looks like someone needs to get her cranky-ass laid."

"Oh, shut up," I snap. "I can't believe Race thought I'd share a room with him." Well, actually, I can. He's the kind of control freak who'd try something like this and expect me to thank him for it.

"Well, I think it's sexy."

"*What?*" I drag my hands through my hair, my frustration that my supposed bestie is siding with my nemesis increasing as my fingers snag in travel-knots. "He's just trying to play me again. All this bullshit about being in love. The man's certifiable if he thinks I'll fall for that crap."

Casey folds her arms beneath her Anorak sweater-covered breasts, the only busty woman alive who can pull off the look without puffing up like the Michelin Man. "What if he means it?"

"Love doesn't exist. Not for a man like him. He's all about business, business, business and doing whatever it takes to make himself rich." I pull off my gloves and toss them onto a dresser made entirely of crystal clear ice.

"I wasn't talking about love," she says, plopping onto the edge of the bed with a little bounce. "I was talking about him wanting to fuck you into bliss. Whooo…" She fans herself with her hand. "That's pretty hot."

"No it's not. It's demented. Just like this whole screwed-up situation. Which, I might add, is entirely *your* fault." I wave off her wide-eyed look and the guilt, which tinges the edges of it, and press forward with a stab of my middle finger in her direction. "Signing on with Race's company to produce the *Steam Bunny* cartoon show was one thing. But did you have to let him take over your wedding too? You don't even *like* weddings."

Turning Casey's and Lucas's wedding into a reality TV show. *Holy hell.* That has to be one of the stupidest PR stunts I've ever heard of. I could kill Race for putting them up to it. All the attention makes me want to scream, but as Casey's maid-of-honor, I've been dragged right into the middle of it—and the inescapable clutches of Race Lindstrom.

Casey smiles, and it's that one she's used since a kid to get an extra helping of dessert at dinner, or more recently, to turn Lucas's brain to mush and get him to agree on stupid things like this wedding show fiasco. "Have I or haven't I hooked you up with the ultimate all-expenses paid trip to Sweden? We've got the Northern Lights, awesome food," she holds up a chocolate dipped strawberry from a bowl chilling on the nearby night table as evidence, "and a kick-ass party at the most romantic place ever, the Ice Hotel. It's a freakin' paradise!" She pops the strawberry into her mouth with a wink.

Unwelcome memories of the last time I ate strawberries with Race seeps into my mind as I watch her chew and swallow, and I find it suddenly hard to breathe. "I wouldn't call sleeping on a slab of ice paradise," I mutter. I stamp my feet slightly, wishing I'd worn thick pants instead of a skirt and leggings. The air is necessarily cold to keep the hotel from melting, but does it have to be *this* cold? If my fingers get any more chilled, I'll have to wear my gloves to bed.

"Who said anything about sleeping?" She laughs, a husky chortle which has turned men's heads since we were teenagers. "Look. I know it's all rushed and you had to scramble to get the time off work, but this is the last weekend the Ice Hotel is open this season. They've extended it just for us. If we don't do this now, we won't get another chance to check out the venue until next year, and we need the preliminary footage for the show."

"Who ever said I wanted to come to Sweden?" I haven't ever, in fact. Despite my grandparents having been born here, and my parents offering to send me for a visit several times, I've never been. The idea has always seemed…oddly unsettling, actually, a feeling that's stabbing at me as I contemplate what's ahead of me now.

A weekend trapped in ice and snow with the biggest jerk I've ever met, and hoo-boy, I've met some big-ass jerks in my life. I seem to be a magnet for them. But Race Lindstrom, Mr. Hot-shot Producer and Serial Seducer? He takes the crown.

Handsome is as handsome does, my mother always said. Yeah? So what genetic defect have I been born with which makes it impossible for me to listen?

One look at Race across that crowded convention room four weeks ago, and I fell for his sexy smile. Instant fatal attraction.

Boom.

Problem is, no matter how much I try, I can't seem to un-fall for him. Despite the fact he used me and slept with me to get a business contract with my friends, there's always a tiny treacherous part of me that craves him. Just thinking of him causes an ache deep in my chest. And if he's in the same room? The ache consumes my insides, reminding me that I've never been the same since meeting him. A piece of my soul is missing when he isn't around, and I get irritable and anxious and become the annoying She-beast From Horny Hell that I am now.

The plane ride was unbearable with him sitting so near and raking me with his hungry stares. I've wanted nothing more than to forget he exists, but as I stand here glaring at Casey, all I can think of is Race.

Fuck.

What is wrong with me? Why do I have to be so attracted to a lying dickhead?

The chiseled planes of his features, the little dimple on his chin, the wicked look in his sexy-as-sin blue eyes—oh, hell, those eyes. Slightly slanted like a cat's and rimmed with thick brown lashes, they make my pulse race when he looks at me, talks to me, says my goddamned name.

Ahhh-strid.

Forget him being tall and muscular with the body of a sex-god, that Scandinavian accent of his plays like erotic music in my ears. He rolls each syllable in his mouth as if my name is something to be savored.

With a shake of her head and twitch of her lips, Casey breaks our glaring match. "Well, whatever. *I'm* glad we're here. And Lucas is too." She arches a brow and taps the shoe-sized wrapped gift-box sitting innocently next to her on the middle of the bed, the one that I've been doing a great job of ignoring, until now. "Looks like Race left you another present."

"Looks like," I mutter, and turn to rummage through my purse. Somewhere in the depths of the bag I've packed Tylenol, though I doubt it has much hope of alleviating my Race-sized headache.

"Are you going to open it?"

"No." Not any more than I've opened any other gifts he's sent me over the past few weeks. My affection can't be bought.

"Then I am." Snatching up the box, Casey tears at the crisp paper and bow faster than I can let out a startled squeak of protest.

"Casey!" Dropping my bag in frustration, I lunge for her, trying to snatch the box, but she scoots out of my reach across the bed. "Goddamnit! Will you just leave it alone?"

"No," she says, opening the box and tossing white tissue paper aside. "You're being silly and stubborn." Her breath catches in a startled sigh as another sheet of tissue paper floats to the bed and she peers at the contents inside the box. "Well, well, well, someone's going to have a fun weekend after all." She arches a brow, a teasing grin spreading her plump lips wide. "Oh. My. God. Get a load of this."

My mouth goes dry as she lets the box drop to the bed and slowly pulls out the contents: a sturdy-looking pair of golden bracelets.

Oh. My. God, indeed.

The bracelets glint innocently enough in the artificial star light, but at about two inches long and made to wrap about the wrist with velvet-lined snugness, they are a striking reminder of the ones I wore while dressed up as Amazon Woman for Race. Those were plastic instead of finely-crafted jewelry, but the coincidence is, well, knowing Race, probably not a coincidence at all.

Role-play was just a word to me before that infamous weekend. I was at the Fan Expo convention to help Casey and Lucas sell their books, but mostly to help them patch up their relationship. And yeah, okay, I was more than a bit lonely watching them kiss and make up and be so much in love.

When Race arrived, I jumped at the spur-of-the moment adventure he offered. Spell bound at first sight of him, I didn't care what lurked behind his Bat Guy mask. He made me feel special. Cherished. Alive. His taste and scent set me on fire. And the feel of his big, strong hands as they caressed my body reverently, then held me tight while he fucked the best orgasms of my life out of me? Yeah, the glow from that will stay with me forever.

Taking the bracelets from Casey, I toss them onto the bed, using the motion to cover up the tears which prickle my eyes as I think of how good things should be.

No matter how I might try to deny it, four weeks of only battery-operated pleasure is no substitute for what I shared with Race. That weekend with him was filled with the best sex I've ever had. I tried things with him I've never tried before. He opened up a whole new world of pleasure that I ache for night and day.

Which is why I'm so pissed that he ruined everything by being a lying prick.

I foolishly thought he was interested in me. Stupid jackass was really after nailing a business deal with Casey and Lucas. But I showed him who was boss in the end. He deserved every moment of humiliation he received when I left him butt naked in the hotel room, tied up with my Amazon Woman Rope of Reality.

Casey's green eyes widen as she caresses the smooth metal bracelets with her fingers. "Is that real gold?"

"Probably." I sigh.

The first time I was with Race, he pinned me against a wall with bracelets just like those. And I can't suppress the shiver of excitement that ripples down my spine as I imagine him doing the same again. I want to experience the anticipation that consumes me as I wait, unable to move, wondering when and where his hot, demanding lips will touch me first.

Shit.

I take a step backward as my body and soul shake with the desire filling me to hunt him down and fuck him hard. It's all I can think about since getting off the plane, and it's really pissing me off to be so needy for him.

Casey looks at me sharply. Concern quickly replaces her teasing smile. "What's wrong?"

"Nothing." How can I explain to her what I can't even explain to myself?

She arches a brow. "Your hands are shaking."

I ball them into fists to stop the tremors rippling from my core. "Seriously, it's nothing. I'm just tired from travelling." But I know she doesn't believe me. We've known each other too long, so I press on, "Why don't you take the bracelets. Lucas will know what to do with them."

At the mention of her favorite man, the smile is back on her lips. But she shakes her head. "Honest to God, all I feel like right now is a nap."

And I'm instantly beside her on the bed, feeling like a massively selfish bitch. I've been so consumed with my own frustration that I haven't given a thought to my best friend. "You okay? The Baby Bunnies aren't making you sick again, are they?"

"Baby Bunnies," she says with a soft smile. "God, I still can't believe I'm having twins." After lifting up the hem of her sweater to see her stomach, she pats her belly. Barely twelve weeks along and she's already starting to show a small bump there.

But as I touch my fingers to her warm abdomen, I close my eyes and I can hear them. "Two little heartbeats, racing fast and strong." Love and warmth rush through me, knowing my bestie and her babies are fine. I smile as I open my eyes and catch her looking at me, her gaze sparkling bright with happiness and more than a little curiosity.

"Tell me again how you can hear that when I can't?" she asks.

"Some people are more sensitive to these things," I say, moving my hand away from her skin. It's what I've always told myself anyway, to explain the peculiarities of my life, but during the past month since meeting Race, I've begun to wonder if there isn't something more to it.

Sarahkka. In ancient Sami culture, she's a respected goddess of childbirth. You remind me of her.

His words whisper though my mind with the same prickle of awareness and apprehension they did when he teased me about it the day we met at the convention. All the stupid *my goddess* crap. I assumed he was joking. I mean, yeah, I've always been a little different with certain things. Like knowing when a guy is healthy and clean so I don't need him to wear a condom when I cave to the loneliness aching inside me. And being able to predict pregnancy one hundred percent of the time. I should be working at a fertility clinic. I could take bets and win money to donate to a teenage-mom-to-be fund or something.

What's it going to be, Astrid? Pink or blue? Ha, ha, ha.

I quickly snatch that escaping sliver of memory and shove it back inside the box in my mind. I don't want to relive that pain again. Because just like I can feel the little hearts beating, I can also feel them die. I've learned the hard way to be careful. Not leave anything to chance. Quarterly shots so I don't ever get pregnant again. My faith is in chemical science to shut out the demons screaming inside.

But seriously, I'm not any more special than anyone else. Like Casey being kick-ass at marketing or Lucas an awesome artist. We all have our talents. This goddess stuff is just crap that Race is using to dig at me. At least, that's what I want to believe. Because it's easier than thinking that somehow he knows my fears and wants to bring them alive.

"Lucas is so proud," I say to distract myself as much as Casey. "I love the way he's strutting around. You're lucky, you know." A familiar pang of jealousy creeps through me about the love she and Lucas share. That kind of relationship doesn't happen for just anyone. It certainly hasn't ever happened for me.

She lowers her sweater and smooths it over her belly. "Yeah, I am lucky. And just think, I almost tossed it all away because I was too afraid to trust him."

"You do have a habit of being a stubborn biatch," I tease.

She cocks one of her immaculate brows. "Takes one to know one."

Ignoring the pointed reference to my own current love-life predicament, I turn the subject. "You sure you're up for all this crazy publicity shit?"

"I'm fine. The nausea isn't so bad today. I really am just tired." She yawns and pats my knee, and I can see the dark circles beneath her eyes that make-up doesn't quite hide. "I think I'll head back to my room and see if I can get in a rest before tonight's party. Lucas said something about a massage," she says with a not-very-subtle wink.

I grin. "In that case, I'll see you *much* later. I need to get my room changed anyway. No way in hell am I staying here with *him*."

Casey's brow furrows a bit as she studies me. "You know, Astrid. I get that he pissed you off with the whole Bat Guy deception thing. Hell, he pissed me off for doing it, too. But, why are you really angry? Did he do something else to you? Something you think I can't handle?"

And, instantly, the gulf between us that's been building for weeks becomes a giant crevasse filled with words I'm afraid to say. A line I cannot cross for fear of sounding insane. Yes, he did do something to me. He awoke something in me when he fucked me. A hunger for him so strong I cry his name at night, screaming for him in my dreams. An awareness that this world around me isn't the one I thought I knew, and it freaks me the fuck out.

He made my clothes disappear while I was wearing them.

Not as in taking them off, I mean *disappear*. As in, *poof*. I was blindfolded at the time, but I felt the surge of energy pulse through him, and I *know*. Even though he hasn't ever said, and those self-same clothes were neatly folded on the bed for me in the morning. I *know* it happened. I didn't imagine it in the heat of passion, though I wish that were the case. Because as impossible as it sounds, he broke the laws of physics and shattered my reality too. I've always taken comfort in the fact that the sun would rise and set each day, and rain would fall from clouds. The constancy of nature is a dependable thing…but maybe not with Race Lindstrom around.

He isn't a regular guy. And I'm caught between feeling excited, intrigued and terrified at the prospect. I can't even guess what that means other than I'm attracted to the fact that he's much more than he seems.

What if I'm like that too?

I shake my head, denying the words that stab at me with their unwanted question, and shove the whole issue aside. "It's fine. I'm fine," I insist. "He's just a regular jerk." *I wish.*

And when Casey's expression stiffens, I wish I were a better liar, too. My heart squeezes tight as her eyes fill with sadness that I've shut her out again.

She gives a little nod and looks away. "Well, you're a big girl. I'm sure you know what you're doing. You'll be okay by yourself for a bit?"

I lick my lips and force words past them that sound fake even to my own ears. "Of course. I'll catch you later, okay?"

She gives me a quick hug. "Text me when you're ready to go to the party, yeah?"

"Yeah."

After she leaves, I sit on the bed and watch the rhythmic waves of the Northern Lights arc around the silent room, an ugly ache settling in my chest.

Things between us have changed. We've been BFF's since children. Played with dolls, whispered about periods, cried over boys. Now, she has Lucas and twin babies in her world, and I have…I don't even know what I have. Words can't name what I feel as I sit here, poised on the brink of something I'm terrified of happening, yet am unable to stop as I think of Race.

I've been reckless with trying to fill up the empty space that's always been in my life. Time and time again. Let my desires lead me into relationships that started out hot and exciting, but had no substance. Lust is not love. I've learned that much at least.

And now there is Race. My latest mistake.

A man who makes my heart pound just thinking his name.

A man I can't seem to escape.

The whisper of him is everywhere. In my thoughts, in the memory of his hot breath against my skin, his moan of pleasure in my ears. The way he touched me and knew exactly what pleased me, to the point I passed out from the all-consuming bliss.

'Bliss, sweetheart. I'm going to give you fucking bliss or die trying.'

"Stop it!" I hiss to the empty air, closing my eyes against the fierce need burning through me to unclench my fingers, sneak them beneath my skirt, and press them against my swollen clit. "He can't be in love with me. It's *bullshit*. And I sure as hell am not fucking in love with him."

Rising from the bed, I grab my suitcase and hunt for my workout clothes.

I need to run. A good jog always helps when I'm stressed. Usually, I do a turn on my treadmill, or go for a round of kick-boxing at the gym. A run in the snow will cool me down. Bring some focus. Some peace.

But I know that even if I jog a thousand miles, it will never be enough distance from Race.

Chapter 3
ASTRID

The first snowball whistles past my ear, disintegrating into a splatter of icy crystals with a *thunk* against the solid tree trunk near me.

"What the hell?" For a second, I freeze mid-stride. It's a moment that spells my doom. The second snowball lands square on my ass with a stinging slap.

Shit.

I quickly dodge sideways into the tree line of the path I've been jogging on and turn, looking for my assailant. "Is that all you've got, Race?" I call out into the stillness, my heart beating in my ears like a drum.

It has to be him. Until the snowball's arrival, I haven't heard anyone behind me. Not for ages. The forest has been silent, except for the rhythmic pounding of my feet as I beat my frustration into the icy ground, taking side trail after side trail to who knows where. Hell, maybe. I don't really care. 'Cause after all that running, my frustration hasn't gone away one little bit.

Everything reminds me of Race. The wild wintery forest smells, the wind, the trees. Every damned thing. Coming out here was a mistake. I've surrounded myself with him.

The path, of course, is empty. But I can feel him watching me. Maybe he's been there all the time. Trailing me.

The coward.

Keeping myself hidden as much as possible behind a small copse of birch trees, I dust snow off my stinging ass before it becomes numb. Now that I've stopped jogging, my Lululemon pants, even with leggings beneath, are a thin cover against the subzero temperature.

Peeking around the trunk of the tree, I glance down the rows of pines and cedars bracketing the trail, searching the shadows for him again. A gentle whisper of wind moves the tall tops of the bushy, green-needled pines, but close to the ground not a branch stirs. The only footprints on the trail are mine, but he could be hiding anywhere.

Reaching down with my gloved hands to gather a snowball of my own, I—

The third ball whizzes just above my head and hits the cedar bush beside me, causing a scattering of snow to fall from the branches. It covers my head and neck in a dusting of cold, icy prickles.

"Shit." A hot gasp sears my lungs as I quickly brush the snowflakes off of my hat and cheeks, my heart stuttering with shock and more than a bit of irritation. A stew of emotions thickens as I blink melting snow from my lashes and see him finally.

He seems to materialize from the shadows as he steps out from the line of trees and into a patch of late-afternoon sunlight. Dressed in all-black snow gear, including a hat and gloves. No wonder I didn't see him before. But maybe I wouldn't have anyway, even if he'd been wearing pink polka dots. Except for the fact his boots leave prints in the trail, he seems almost otherworldly, a man made of light and darkness. The enigmatic spirit of the forest clings to him as he walks towards me, lazily tossing another snowball into the air with one hand and catching it again.

"Do you know what happens to people who go alone in a forest?" he calls out.

My heart rate speeds up, even as I try to relax. But it's useless with him so near and that sexy voice of his.

"They get picked on by creepy stalkers?" I snap back as I throw my ball of snow at him.

He stares, lips twitching in amusement as it lands harmlessly on the packed snow trail at his feet.

Well, shit. Baseball has never been my sport of choice.

But his amusement is gone as his piercing, blue-eyed gaze settles on me again. "This was dangerous, Astrid."

"Starting a snowball fight with me? I agree." I bend and grab another handful of snow to make into a weapon. Annoyingly, my fingers are trembling; my whole body is, but not from fear or the cold.

He is coming nearer.

And the fucked-up, horny-she-bitch-from-hell part of me really, really likes it. I can't help staring as he casually strolls down the path toward me. His winter jacket and pants do nothing to hide his strong body, and his presence fills the silence of the woods with his fierce, domineering intensity—an intensity that is completely focused on me.

A traitorously large part of me likes the power he wields, and the way it makes my nipples hard and my knees weak. But the clinging bit of self-preservation that I have left jabs me into motion. I toss my ball of snow at him.

This time it lands on his chest in a messy *whack*. But my joy in hitting my target dies before it's born. He hasn't stopped walking. And that intense stare is still trained on me. Panic floods me as I bend to scoop up some more snow to try and pelt him with—

My hand jerks back, stinging from the sudden impact of his hard snowball against my glove.

"Goddammit, Race. What do you want?"

"You frightened me," he says in the same cool tone. But as he draws near, sparks of fire burn in his cobalt eyes.

"I what?" I stare at him dumbfounded.

"Why didn't you wait at the hotel?"

"For you?"

He pauses in his advance as if I've struck him. "Do you see anyone else out here?" He gestures around at the wall of trees. The only sound is the creak and groan of sleeping branches caressed by the wind.

The wind. Has it picked up since I began my jog? How many hours ago?

I check my phone. I've been gone less than an hour and half, lost in thought, mostly jogging, sometimes walking. The well-worn path started out along the shoreline of a river by the Ice Hotel. But since then the trees have thickened, and the snowpack deepened into undisturbed trail. No one has come this way all day. Except for me. And Race.

The chill was barely noticeable when I started, but now, as I stand here gawping at him, it's seeping into my booted feet and spreading up my legs.

"Come on," he says, moving close enough to grasp my arm. "The sun will be setting soon. It gets cold here after dark. And there are…wild animals."

"Animals?" I ask suspiciously. Come to think of it, I don't recall hearing any animals. Not even a bird, which is kind of weird. But I try to ignore the sensation of warmth that his tight grip brings me. "You mean the kind who stalk women and throw snowballs at them from the trees? *Hey!* You don't have to yank my arm off. I can take care of myself."

"Really?" he snaps, not lessening his grip. If anything, it tightens as he hauls me away from the birch trees and back onto the path. I dig in my heels, uncomfortable with the arousing effect his nearness is having on me as much as the fact I'm being manhandled.

I'm not a doll. A piece of ass to be lugged around at will. And I've vowed to never again be pushed around by a guy, especially this one. Not after everything I've gone through before with other men. I bent over backwards to make my last relationship work, and Paul-the-prick cheated on me anyway. Is deceitfulness inevitable when it comes to men? The guys I've met want only one thing, and it isn't freakin' love.

Sticking my foot out, I catch him in the back of his knee with the toe of my boot. As he instinctively bends off balance, I pull his arm backward and flex my own, drawing him close to my body.

A quick flip over my shoulder, and he's sprawled on the ground in a puff of snow and a surprised, "*Oomph.*"

"Really," I say, looking down at his startled face. *Take that, jerkwad.* I can't resist smirking as I dust off my gloved hands and turn to walk down the path.

As I step forward, his steel grip flexes about my ankle, snagging me and dragging me backward. I land on my knees, hard, the impact jarring my wrists and up my arms as I try to stop from slamming face-down into the snow.

Adrenalin has me scrambling, twisting onto my back to try and escape his grip, but he is quicker. Crawling over my body, he pins me to the ground, pressing me down into the snow with his weight. I buck and struggle, grasp a loose fistful of the white ice crystals, intent on throwing it in his face to blind him.

He clamps one of his strong hands around my wrists, pulls my arms above my head, and holds me tight against the ground. It's a parody of the way he held me the first time we fucked against his hotel room wall. I enjoyed it then. I will not enjoy it now.

At least that's what I want to believe.

But the truth is I'm so turned on by our struggles and his big, hard body commanding mine that I can barely breathe.

His eyes are hot blue stars, burning into mine, and I know by the look of heart-stopping desire in them that there is no escape. Not for either of us. My throat becomes a lump as I suck in his primal, alpine scent.

"Astrid," he says with a yearning whisper as the tips of his gloved fingers brush my cheek. The gentle touch stirs all kinds of sensations zinging through me to my core. "My beautiful goddess."

Fuck. Not this goddess shit again.

"Don't call me that!" Panic-tinged anger and a whole lot of heat burns through my limbs. I try again to loosen his grip and buck him off, but only succeed in pushing myself farther into the soft-packed snow. "Let go of me, you ass!"

"No."

I grit my teeth against his calm smugness and reach for a more persuasive tone. "Come on, Race. I'm cold."

"I'm not." His hot breath fans across my cheek as he wedges himself more firmly between my thighs. The hard ridge of his thick cock is unmistakable, even hidden within all the layers of protection against the cold. His eyelids flutter shut as a slight grimace crosses his chiseled features "Ah, damn, you fit me so good, baby. We were meant to be together."

"Bullshit."

He grinds into me. "Does this feel like bullshit to you?" His mouth moves toward my lips, but I turn my face aside, despite the pleasure racing through my veins.

"What? You mean you didn't get one of your little sluts to help you with that in Kiruna? There were at least ten to choose from when we got off the plane."

His lids lower slightly as he studies me. "You think I can ever be with another woman once I've been with you?"

"You can't expect me to believe you haven't had sex with anyone in almost a month," I scoff.

"Why not?"

"You're too good-looking. You can have any woman you want."

He laughs, a deep rumble that passes through his chest and into me. "Really? Good. Wrap your legs around me, baby."

"Except *me*," I squeak as he shoves my legs apart and rubs his hardness against my soft sex.

My vision goes out of focus with the burst of pleasure that ripples through me. I bite my lip to stifle a groan. I'm sure he must smell how turned on I am. But with my legs now free, I have a choice. Do as he says and wrap myself around him and enjoy this erotic ride, or push my feet against the ground and shove him the hell off.

But I can't seem to move at all as he pins me with his knowing gaze. His breath is a hot, minty fan across my face, causing me to crave the taste of those sculpted lips of his, hovering just above mine.

"You can't tell me you haven't been thinking about me every day for the last month," he murmurs and slips his free hand beneath my head. He cradles it, holding it steady as his mouth dips down. Pressing his lips against mine in a kiss that feels annoyingly brief, he nuzzles a warm trail across my cheek toward my ear.

"Sure." I gasp and flex my wrists in his strong grip, but I no longer know if I'm struggling to get away from him or closer. "I've been thinking about how obnoxious you are. How much you enjoy twisting people up with your lies. How you made my freakin' clothes disappear!"

We both become still as that last accusation bursts free. With a nip to my earlobe, he raises his head and looks me in the eye again, studying me, assessing.

My heart pounds a furious beat as the silence builds. "Say something, you freak!"

"You're shivering," he asserts with a small, calm nod as if I've not just said anything insane.

"What?"

"I don't want you to get sick," he adds ignoring my confused tone.

He moves his free hand from where it cups my head, and skims his fingers through the air just above my body. His eyes become unfocussed as he whispers a word I can't quite hear. But where his hand passes, warmth envelopes me, chasing away any chill from the snow.

"What are you doing?" I ask, a tiny gasp escaping my parted lips from the pleasure of the sensation he's somehow stirring. I feel like I'm on a cushion of heat, and he's the furnace fueling it.

His gaze refocuses as he glances at me with a bemused twist to his lips. "I'm thickening the air particles between you and the ground, to create a barrier against the snow and keep in your body heat."

"You can do that?" I whisper, my heart thudding in my ears as all of the peculiarities about him and me that I've wanted to be imaginary become spoken truths.

He stares down at me, unblinking. "Yes."

I swallow hard. "What else can you do?"

"This," he says. That devastating smile of his splits his lips, and it's as if the sun has come out from behind a cloud, making my stomach flutter in an excited way I'd rather not think about.

But I don't have the chance to think about anything anyway because, faster than I can blink, he lets my wrists go and moves down my body to my spread legs. In the next heartbeat, his mouth is pressed against my groin, his hot breath searing my sex.

"Oh, *fuck!*" I scream, my cry echoing in the woods as I arch my back off the ground in a rictus of intense pleasure.

He's relentless as he cups my hips in his strong hands, his mouth tugging on the tight layers of fabric separating him from me. I wish that he would make them disappear, baring me to him, but he doesn't, not this time. Instead, he uses the abrasion of the fabric to heighten the friction of his tongue and teeth as he nibbles at my clit.

I can't tell if the wetness between my legs is from the intense arousal seeping between my folds or from his mouth. But when he sucks on my pussy and moans at the taste, I begin to come.

I flail and jerk, not caring if anyone might be near, as he drags me closer to the edge and the bliss he's promised on the other side. All I want is the fire that flows from him and into me as he bites on my swollen clit.

It hits me fast and hard. Too fast, but I can't stop it. The intense white light takes me, cocoons me in the warmth of the air that cushions my straining body. The absolute, mind numbing pleasure is better than my dreams. I've craved this connection with him from the deepest part of my soul. And I don't hold back as I grasp his hair in my hands and clutch his face to me, screaming my surrender into the wind and trees.

"*Race!*"

Chapter 4
RACE

She doesn't stir as I carry her back to our room at the Ice Hotel, and only murmurs softly as I undress her and cover her in the warm duvet. Not surprising. She came so hard I'm amazed she's still in one piece. My goddess has missed me as much as I've missed her, whether she wants to admit it or not.

As I lie next to her on the bed, the blissful way she said my name echoes through my mind, making me almost jizz myself with the ravaging need clawing through me. I've longed for weeks to hear her say it with that note of absolute ecstasy. Hearing it pass over her lips in utter abandonment, seconds before passing out from the bliss of the orgasm I gave her, makes the ache to fuck her a feral need I find nearly impossible to resist.

But I want her to be awake when I bury my cock inside her tightness. I need to see her surrender as the pleasure takes her.

Bringing my fingers to my nose, I inhale deeply. My smile widens, my cock becoming even harder from the aroma of pure, unadulterated Astrid. Her scent is still on my skin from when she gushed her delicious honey-warm pleasure into my mouth and on my hands, soaking my gloves.

As I wrap my fingers around Mjolnir, my sensitive cock, it twitches slightly. My hammer is ready to start banging, but I'm torn between letting her rest and waking her up so I can fuck her into senselessness all over again.

I love how soft she looks asleep. The gentle rise and fall of her chest, the puff of air between her plump, parted lips. There isn't a wrinkle of worry anywhere on her beautiful face. She's relaxed. At peace.

A far cry from the tormented woman I know her to be. The one I watched jogging through the forest, muttering to herself, pissed that she couldn't find a different room to be in than the one she has with me. Naively ignoring the obvious danger of being alone in the woods in a foreign place. None of my people will harm a hair on her head, and animals know better than to interfere, but stranger things lurk beneath those trees than wild animals. Spirits attracted to the natural power born in people like her and me.

But the spirits stayed well-hidden as I trailed behind her, making sure she was safe while she worked through the demons spurring her on. When I realized she was taking a path of trails that lead toward my house, I had to intervene.

One day I'll take her to my ancestral home, but we aren't there yet with our trust. I'm certain how she will react to seeing the dark truths that haunt me, and it won't be pleasant. As much as I enjoy the chase, I don't want to make her run from me again.

Tasting her juices as she comes hard, and watching her pass out from the bliss, now that's a much better way to work through our issues.

I reach for her, unable to wait any longer. At the same time, her phone buzzes where I've left it for her on the night table. Her eyelids flutter as she stirs, so I let my hand drop back to the covers.

A low groan escapes her throat while she stretches and blearily reaches for her phone.

"Go away, Casey," she mumbles as she looks at the screen with one eye still closed, and then drops the phone back to the night table unanswered. She sags against the pillows with a sigh, both eyes popping open wide when she notices me next to her.

"Jesus, fuck." She rubs the sleep from her lids with the heels of her hands and blinks at me as she quickly comes fully awake. Her gaze freezes on my groin. She can't seem to get past my exposed, erect dick, which I'm slowly stroking.

"Do you have to be naked?"

"I'm not a big fan of clothes," I reply.

"No kidding." She takes a quick peek beneath the duvet, and a blush spreads up her neck and into her cheeks. "Did you make mine go *poof* again, or take them off with your hands?"

"My hands. Sometimes my teeth. I wasn't in a hurry."

She closes her eyes for a moment and swallows hard before looking at me again. Her eyes track the movement of my hand as I slowly rub my palm up and down the tight skin of my cock. It's agonizing and intensely pleasurable to touch myself and have her watch. I know how much it turns her on.

"I passed out again, didn't I," she mutters matter-of-factly. "How the *hell* do you do that to me?"

I can't help laughing, despite the warning tone of irritation in her voice. I love the fiery way she tries to fight me. And the fact she's starting to accept that I may be a freak, but I'm a freak she can't get enough of.

"Would you like me to show you again?"

"Oh, *God*," she moans and thumps her head against her pillow. "Are you serious?" But she's smiling for the first time since she agreed to this trip, and my cock swells even tighter.

"I want to fuck you senseless, Astrid. Every second. Every day." There's a slightly desperate edge to my ragged tone that makes her look at me with narrowed eyes. The smile slips from her lips again.

"You've seriously not been with anyone else since me?" she asks skeptically, her hands fisting in the duvet. Her gaze drifts toward my cock again and widens as my erection jerks slightly to the pulse of my heavily beating heart.

I stop stroking my dick and lift her chin with my index finger, pinning her eyes to mine so she can see the truth of my words.

"No. I have not pursued, slept with, or in any way fucked anyone else since I met you."

I know she has trust issues. She's been hurt in the past, and not just by me. It's made her wary and selective with her lovers. She hasn't been looking for a fuck buddy during the last four weeks either, which is good. Because if any horny asshole had come near her, I would have fucking killed him.

But her brow furrows with confusion as she studies me, trying to divine the truth. "Why? And don't say it's because you love me," she adds quickly. "Why would you deny yourself?"

Keeping her gaze pinned to mine, I brush my thumb across her full bottom lip. "In order for me to deny myself something, I would have to want it in the first place."

She stares at me incredulously. Her hand covers mine and she gives my thumb a little nip before pushing it away. "Are you trying to tell me that with all the sexy bimbos throwing themselves at you, you haven't wanted *any* of them?"

"Astrid. I'm a powerful man with more money than most people can dream of. Everywhere I go, there are always women and men wanting to fuck me. It's a reality of my life that will never change. But do I *want* them? No."

"Wait a minute. Men?"

"Does it surprise you that men find me attractive?"

She looks me up and down, taking in the full measure of my nudity. That adorable blush I crave creeps up her neck from beneath the duvet. "Well, no. I mean, you're incredible to look at. It's just that…wow." She licks her lips and I can see her thoughts churning.

I wait for her to ask. It doesn't take long.

"So, have you been with a…um, guy, then?"

"Have you been with a woman?"

"*What?* No!" she squeaks her eyes widening with embarrassment as she turns crimson. "Of course not."

But she does like to watch. I've seen the way she looks at her best friend and her fiancé, and I know she enjoys the fact Casey has magnificent tits that bounce and jiggle when getting fucked by Lucas. Getting Astrid comfortable enough to admit it, however, will take some time. But it will help if I level the ground for her a bit.

"I've never fucked another man," I admit. "But I have let guys suck me off, occasionally, if they really wanted to."

Her brows lift upwards. "Did you enjoy it?"

"Not so much."

She seems pleased by that. Her lips purse as she studies me. "So, you prefer women?"

"No. I prefer you," I say and move closer to her. The blush staining her neck is warm to my touch and trails down beneath the duvet, between her pert breasts.

She swallows hard. "Last I checked, I'm pretty sure I'm a woman."

I shake my head as I guide my hands over her curves and peel back the duvet, exposing her down to her waist. I've created a bubble of warmth in the room, to protect her from the chill, but even so, her pale pink nipples instantly pebble as the air touches them. She's so exquisite, it makes my chest ache. "You're a goddess."

She tenses. I know she has hang-ups about her own nudity, but I'm betting her anxiety has more to do with what I've said than done. While she might be willing to toy with the reality that I have some interesting talents, she is still struggling to embrace the reason for her own.

For a second I think she's going to shove me away and storm out the room. But as she sucks in a deep breath, the tension in her body eases a bit. She moves her hand to my left shoulder and hesitantly traces the birthmark imprinted there that's shaped like a deer antler.

"What is this really all about, Race?" Her voice is soft as she follows the branching pattern with the tips of her fingers. "I know I haven't been imagining it all. These things that you can do. They aren't normal." Her eyes dart to mine, challenging me to deny her claim.

Her feather-light touch on my shoulder burns like sweet fire, flaring all the way to my aching groin. I want to pin her to the bed and thrust myself inside her slick heat. But I've been waiting for this conversation to happen for weeks, until she was ready to ask me these things. So I stay stock still and let her trace erotic fire over my skin with her nails and steel myself for a walk down memory lane.

I manage what I hope is a calm smile as I say, "Actually, it is normal. Sometimes people are born with more power than others and it makes them seem special. But inside here, we are all the same." I tap my finger on her chest, between her soft breasts.

Her long blond hair plays about her shoulders as she shakes her head. "I don't understand."

"I didn't for a long time either," I admit as I lazily trace my fingers along her collar bone and sweep the tousled strands of hair away from her neck. Her skin is like warm silk. I could caress her for hours and it would never be enough. "My mother explained it to me. She was *noaidi*, which is sort of like a shaman in Sami culture. She passed her training on to me."

Darkness threatens, gnawing at the edges of my soul with the memories I've tried hard to forget. But the inevitable pain fills me as I think of my mother's warm brown eyes and gentle voice. I've lived so long in L.A. I've almost forgotten how vivid the aching is, how coarse and alive it can be. But here, in the place of my birth, it bites with sharp teeth that have no intention of ever letting me go. I can never truly forget what I have done or escape the staggering cost.

I roll over onto my back and prop my hands beneath my head. But staring up at the Northern Lights display flickering on the ceiling only provides a backdrop for my memories to play out on. Maybe I should have picked a different room. This one makes the power flicker through my veins in time with the lights, dancing so close to the truth.

Astrid follows after a moment, arranging herself on her side beside me. Her soft breasts brush against my chest as she leans over to cup my cheek with her hand. "Your mother was a shaman?" she prompts.

Her clear blue eyes are filled with steady confidence, but I wonder how long it will be there when she discovers the darkness haunting my existence. Her soft touch grounds me just the same. She is my salvation. My heart.

"Yes. Or a wise woman. Spirit guide. There is no direct translation to anything you would know it to be. But basically she understood the connection between the land and the spirit, which was a good thing. Because that connection is very strong in me."

Moving one of my hands from behind my head, I rest it over hers, and let the bright sweetness of the touch fill me. It doesn't chase the pain away, but it helps. It's the one thing in the world that does. The source of my addiction to her.

I clear my throat. "The first time it happened, it was a hot summer day. The sky was clear and blue. Not a cloud in sight." She moves her fingers from my cheek and entwines them with mine instead, giving them a little squeeze of encouragement to continue. I answer her small smile with one of my own as I say, "I remember being very small and sitting on her knee, looking up at the sky. How old was I…maybe a year or two?" It's so long ago now, just a blur pieced together with sharp emotions. "I don't know what we were waiting for, just sitting there by the lake in the sun. All I remember is feeling hot. And cranky. My mother didn't understand. She yelled at me…and I got angry."

"Babies fuss all the time. It's normal," Astrid says giving a little shrug. "You should see my cousin's kid. Total demon child. If they ever do a remake of *The Exorcist*, I'm sending in his name." She grins as she settles herself closer against me. Her warm breasts press against my chest as she glances at my massively erect cock.

It juts upward from my groin like a lightning rod, waiting to ignite her. I'm achingly tempted to skip this explanation and just bury myself in her soft heat. But she deserves to know the truth before I fuck her senseless again.

"Yeah, okay. Babies get cranky," I admit. "But I asked the sky to make it rain," I pause, watching her for her reaction. "And it did."

Her gaze snaps from admiring my cock to focusing on my face. "It just…rained?" Her nipples are hard buds, pebbling into my skin. I place my palm against her back and press her closer. Maybe to feel her heat. Maybe to stop her from running away. Maybe because it just feels fucking good to have her here, listening.

"Well, not right away. It took a few minutes for my need to affect the air molecules, but we weren't outside much longer. The storm blew up fast over the lake. My mother grabbed me and took me inside the house. It was a big downpour. Lots of thunder and lightning."

"Were you scared?"

"No. It was exciting." The thrill of it still sizzles through me as I think of that first time. It's a feeling I've never been able to control, not even in the face of wide-eyed terror.

"But your mother must have been freaked out by the things you can do."

"She always understood. She tried to help me learn control. My father, on the other hand, wanted to lock me away."

"People really do that?" There's outrage in her eyes, but I'm pleased to see no pity.

"It was a long time ago."

He's a monster. He's going to hurt someone someday if we don't take care of it now.

You're wrong. He's a gift. Our gift from the gods, Ronnie. I'll never stop loving him. And I'll never let anyone take him away. Not even you.

My lungs feel tight and I blink hard against the brittle memory of my mother's devotion and strength. But Astrid's eyes hold nothing more than clear-headed pragmatism as she gazes steadily at me.

"So you can control the weather," she says matter-of-factly. Her fingers tap against my chest as she considers the idea.

"I can influence it, yes. And other things." I avoid that dangerous explanation by concentrating on her flawless skin as I brush it with my palms. I caress her neck and shoulders in slow, languorous movements, and let the velvet touch anchor me.

"Can you fly?"

"No."

"X-ray vision?"

"No," I laugh, and the tightness inside me eases.

"But…how is this even possible?" she whispers, her pupils wide pools as she shakes her head, trying to understand. And for that fact alone I could love her for a thousand lifetimes, even if I didn't already love her for this one.

"Every culture has its legends," I say as she shivers beneath my caress. "Passed down by songs before they were chiseled into stones. Stories about people who can do incredible things." I push the duvet lower and expose her beautiful, tight ass cheeks. God, she's gorgeous. Fucking beautiful.

"Myth and legend," she chokes out as I smooth my hand over a full globe. Her firm butt is warm against my palm. I give it a squeeze.

"History," I correct as she sucks in a sharp breath. "The history of humanity, born before time. Everyone has something. Something they are good at or can do better than others. A dominant trait that's in their genes. A gift from the gods passed on through each generation, sometimes combining to create new things. Unbelievable things. Like me. And you."

She doesn't say anything and I wait for a moment, letting her absorb what I've said. There's a large part of her that doesn't trust me, but something deep inside must recognize the truth. I squeeze her ass harder, massaging the firm skin.

She bites her lip as she squirms. "You know, that's very distracting."

Rather than say anything, I just keep up the steady ass massage. I want to drive her so insane with lust she'll take in everything I've said without question.

Her eyes narrow and she shakes her head in annoyance. "I'm nothing like you."

"Yes, you are. You have a mark too, hidden in the fold behind your left ear."

"So? Lots of people have birthmarks."

"Shaped like a woman standing inside a house?" The mark of *Sarahkka.*

She pushes away from me and sits up, pressing her hand to her ear as if by doing so she can hide the truth. Her eyes are wide, her breathing sharp. She's getting ready to bolt.

I keep my voice calm as I touch my own reindeer birthmark. "This is a symbol of power, Astrid. A gift given to me from the gods. My mother's Sami blood mixed with Norse from my father. It's very primal and old."

"So you're what? Some sort of god?"

I laugh softly. "No. I'm just a man who happens to make it rain when he's sad and thunder when he's angry."

Her brows flick. "Like Thor?"

I smile. "Something like that."

She looks me up and down, her hot gaze fixing on my very erect, patiently waiting cock. "Well, you know what they say, never judge a guy by the size of his hammer."

A laugh bursts from my throat. "Only the worthy can handle Mjolnir," I warn in mock seriousness.

Her eyes flick to mine. "And am I worthy?" she teases, making my blood boil.

"Hell, yeah."

"Well, that's too bad." she says letting out a pent-up breath of her own. "It's been nice chatting, but I'm going for a shower."

Chapter 5

I push the covers off of me and quickly slip out of the bed, fully expecting him to grab hold of me and fuck me senseless with that steel-hard hammer of his. It's what I want, isn't it? My heart is pounding, my insides quaking with the need to fuck and be fucked so badly I could scream.

But as I hastily walk naked on the fur rug spanning the short distance to the bathroom, I'm keenly aware he hasn't moved an inch. His arm is still crossed beneath his head as he watches my every move. His eyes are heavy-lidded and intense, and an amused grin twists his lips at my pathetic attempt at defiance.

He's a predator biding his time. I know full well I can't escape. I don't even bother to lock the bathroom door behind me. He'll probably just materialize through it anyway or whatever it is that he does.

But I need a precious moment to breathe.

I can't think straight when he's around and I really need to think. His presence is overwhelming. His scent and voice tease my senses more intimately than his hands. Though, holy hell, he knows how to use those too. And that gorgeous cock of his, just waiting for me to fuck it…God. I'm shaking inside with the burning desire to race back out of the shower, grab hold of his cock and suck him off. I crave his taste so badly I ache like an addict. All it will take is one word and I can have my fix. But giving in to that temptation four weeks ago was what started this whole mess. So I flick on the faucet and hope the shower head has a good, vibrating spray to give me some desperately needed relief. That surprise orgasm in the forest still sings through my veins, making me ache for him even more.

I smile as I adjust the temperature. *Mjolnir.* Fuck. He named his dick after Thor's hammer.

And double fuck, he's some sort of freakin' god. Or a demi-god. Or something. I have no idea how that works. And I'm not sure I want to. What I want to believe is that he's being a dick again and that this is all some sort of game. Revenge for me leaving him tied up naked in the hotel room back at that convention. Or for dumping his stuff out in the snow this afternoon. Some sort of normal, predictable plan to make a fool out of me so that he gets the last laugh. I was gullible enough to trust him the first time we met; how fucking funny would it be to get me to trust him now?

But the joke's on him. I'm already a fool.

Because I can't deny the impossible things I've seen him do, or the fact that every time he touches me I slip deeper under his spell.

As I step into the stall and shut the glass door, warm mist begins to swirl around me. I close my eyes and enjoy the feeling of the water cascading over me. The heat is soothing, but I can't relax. My thoughts are still on him and his perfect cock.

And dammit…this shower head doesn't detach.

Where is he, anyway?

When is he going to pounce?

The anticipation is driving me crazy hot. Daggers of need shoot through my veins. I know he's followed me into the bathroom. I can sense him somewhere behind me, watching me through the glass. But I stop myself from turning to look. I won't be able to resist the sight of him standing there naked and aroused. If he wants to watch me playing with myself, then he can damn well watch.

Small bottles of scented soaps are arranged on a shelf beside me in the stall. I choose one whose Swedish name I can't decipher, but the liquid inside smells like elderflower. A shudder grips me as memories flash through my mind. The erotic things Race and I did when he fed me strawberries while I was blindfolded. Those berries were so sweet, and Race…oh, God. His cock tasted amazing, covered with that elderflower flavored whipped cream.

I squeeze a dollop of the creamy soap into my palm and spread it over me, caressing my sensitive breasts and my belly, before moving my hand lower.

The lather feels good as I work it around the soft folds between my legs. My mound is freshly waxed, except for the tuft I always leave above my clit. The different textures of my smooth skin and the coarse hair play against my fingers. It's warm, soft and slippery. I love the way my body feels here. The way I feel when I give it some playtime.

My eyelids drift shut as I gently press my forefinger between the folds, taking care with my swollen and sensitive clit. My tiny nub is hot and throbbing, my heartbeats dancing to the rhythm of the water falling in streams against me.

Steam swirls in the heated air, coalescing around me. I can't help thinking of Race as I touch myself. The way he touches me, gently at times and urgent at others. His hot breath fanning against my cheek as he moans in my ear.

Velvet heat envelopes my nipples like a warm, wet mouth.

My eyes flash open. "What the—" I begin to say, but the rest of my words are lost in a shocked gasp.

The mist is alive with images of Race.

His fingers, made of white vapor that sweeps against my skin. A thousand of his mouths press against my body in soft kisses that caress me everywhere at the same time. Tendrils spear into my hair, caressing my nape, my back. They swirl around my breasts and over my nipples, again and again.

His alpine scent is everywhere. Inside my lungs as I breathe the mist in. Soaking into my skin.

"Holy mother of God," I whisper and brace one hand against the glass wall.

I've never experienced anything like this. His mist-touch is insanely sensual. Insubstantial, but firm and warm at the same time. Overwhelming, but not quite enough. A deep moan escapes my throat at the feeling that's tightening inside me.

I arch my back, thrusting my breasts forward into the steady rain of water. It pounds upon my hard nipples, making them tingle and ache. But the pleasure doesn't feel anywhere nearly as good as what's coming from the mist spilling around me.

His ghost-hands move over my ass, caressing each cheek and touching my thighs with feathery sweeps. Another pair moves between my legs as I part them. His mist-self swirls around my pussy, moving in time with my hand, while embracing the rest of my body in warm Race-scented kisses. It's the most intimate and intensely erotic thing I've ever felt in my life.

My mind blanks to everything else but the need thundering in my veins. I tremble as I move one finger away from my clit and push it up inside my center.

I'm tight, and hot, and slick with arousal. But he's there with me, a gyrating swirl of steam, as I move my hips against my hand. In and out. Seeking more. Deeper.

A thousand velvet tongues slip past my palm and lick my clit. I press my thighs together and lean sideways against the glass, trying hard to keep standing as a shudder wracks my body. I'm aching to come. The mist is intense, but at the same time it's too soft, too gentle.

I want more.

"Race." I gasp his name as the hunger gnaws at me, urging me to fill my pussy with his hard cock instead of my fingers and his phantom essence.

"I'm right here, baby."

As I turn around, I can see him through the mist, standing on the other side of the glass. He's jerking his cock, stroking himself as he watches me enjoy the effects of his supernatural fuckery.

I can't stand it anymore.

I want that cock.

Raging need burns through me in a white-hot flash. My hand slips from between my legs and instinctively presses against the barrier between us, my fingers turning white where the soft pads clutch the glass.

Instantly, he's there, wrapping me in his strong—very real—arms and smothering the ache threatening to unnerve me.

"Use me, baby. Tell me what you want," he murmurs by my ear, his breath warmer and sweeter than the mist.

I clutch at him as if he's a lifeline. His body is a wall of heat that I can't exist without. He trails kisses down my neck, but I'm too aroused for soft comforts. His hard cock presses into my belly, reminding me of a greater need.

"I want to fucking suck you," I say, giving in to the craving I've had since seeing him again on the plane. "I want you to lose your shit all over me." A sense of power fills me as I push away from his embrace and slide down his body onto my knees.

His beautiful cock is hard, the veins running beneath his skin pulsing with his virility. I have done this to him. Aroused him to this point of god-like fortitude. I can toy with him and tease him. He's completely in my control. And he's been waiting for me for nearly four fucking weeks.

"Do you jerk yourself off, thinking of me?" I murmur.

The water spills over his glorious shoulders and down his back, shielding me from the spray as I look up at his chiseled face. His eyes are fever-bright, watching me with intense hunger.

"Yes," he says.

"Do you imagine me doing this?"

A shudder wracks him as I grasp him with my hands and give a quick pump. Long and thick, his cock is gorgeous. *He's* gorgeous. His powerful hips and thighs are all hard muscle, trembling slightly as he steadies himself.

His hands clutch my hair. "When I close my eyes, all I can see is your plump, greedy lips wrapped around my cock. You suck me so good. You fucking shred me, Astrid."

His fingers spear into my wet hair with an urgency that I feel vibrating through his palms and into my soul. I know how much he desperately wants me, and I love the feeling it gives me.

But I can't stop the unwanted image of him that lurks at the back of my mind. Him, letting another person suck him off, and enjoying it. I'm certain he's had hundreds of lovers. How could he not? He's confessed as much. Maybe I'm a bit sensitive from all the cheating losers I've dated. But thinking of Race enjoying this rush with someone else makes something suspiciously close to jealously flare inside me.

"Did you really let some guy do this to you?" I ask then press my mouth over his tip and give it a little suck. He's salty and earthy, just like I remember.

He pulls in a sharp breath and studies me, flinching slightly when I flick him with my tongue. He licks his lips as he grimaces. "There was a time when it seemed like a solution to my problems."

I pause in my stroking. "Solution? That sounds very clinical."

"Yes."

But what we're doing right now isn't. And the tight knot of jealousy loosens. I have no idea what his fucked-up story is, and I'm not sure I want to. But pain is etched in his voice and mirrored in the soulful ache burning from his eyes. He's filled with a deep loneliness that echoes mine. It's an emptiness that has never been filled, except when I'm with him.

Does it really matter who he's fucked or how he's experimented in the past? Something or someone has hurt him. He probably deserved it for being a manipulative ass. But right now I'm consumed with the need to burn away whatever memory has him bleeding inside. Show him that whoever's lips have made him come in the past, will never be as good as mine.

Because he's right.

In this moment, he is mine. Mine to fuck. Mine to use. He's given me complete control. I feel light headed. Maybe from the heat of the water and steam, maybe from him and what he's doing to me.

His thick cock pushes deep into my throat, then pulls back out as he pumps himself between my lips. His gaze narrows, his jaw clenching from the pleasure of being where he's been denied for so many weeks.

I moan from the absolute bliss filling me. I want to see him lose control and come all over me. His hot spray flooding my mouth and coating my skin.

The clever tendrils of mist swirl about me, passing between my legs and tickling the inside of my thighs. It feels so good, I spread my knees to give him better access. My supernatural lover. My sexy god. He's all I've craved for weeks. All I've dreamed about since we met, maybe before that if I want to be really honest with myself.

But I don't want to look too closely at the pleasure being here like this gives me. All I know is that whatever he is, he's real.

And right now, he's mine.

Keeping one hand wrapped around his cock as he pumps himself in my mouth, I let the other play with his heavy balls. He jerks in response, his muscular thighs flexing as he moans. I catch his gaze and see the way his pupils widen as the pleasure rushes through his veins. His lips part on a deep, hungry groan.

"That's it baby. You know how to do it. Suck me off. Suck me hard."

I caress his balls again, and let my fingers play with the sensitive skin between his cock and his ass. He tenses slightly, his fingers digging into my scalp. Does he like it a bit kinky? I don't want to stop to ask. I love the way his cock stretches my lips, as he thrusts inside my mouth.

I move my fingers up along the channel from his balls and between his taut butt cheeks. When I feel his puckered opening, I stop. The water flows down his back and between his flexing ass cheeks, giving me some lube. I tease him with tiny circles, enjoying how his sphincter flexes and pulses as I dance my finger against it.

"Oh fuck, baby. Fuck that's good." He says, holding my head tight as he pumps my mouth. His thighs quiver, his wild eyes watching me. Hungry. Pleading for release. For me to make him come hard.

He's so close, barely hanging on.

I moan as I suck him deep into my throat and press the tip of my finger into his tight sphincter at the same time.

"Goddamn, fuck...*Astrid.*" He grunts as he clenches. His entire body shudders, the fingers in my hair grasping almost painfully as his hot seed gushes. The rush of energy from him rips though me, vaporizing the mist. I lose my balance, but his grip on my hair tightens, stopping me from falling. His pleasure is my pleasure, sizzling through my veins. It fills my mouth with warm spurts as he continues to pump himself between my lips.

I try to swallow it all, but it's too much. His cock pops out of my mouth, and it's my turn to moan as thick ropy tendrils of his come sprays over my chin and down onto my breasts. I close my eyes and just enjoy his musky scent and taste, the feel of his sticky heat as I rub it on my tight nipples. I scoop some on my fingers and rub it on my swollen clit. His seed tingles where it touches me, making me almost come from the bliss. Holy God, how I have missed this. Why the fuck have I denied us this?

"Ah, my goddess," he says, his voice liquid heat. "My beautiful fucking goddess,"

I'm shaking as he lifts me to my feet. How the hell has he kept standing after that powerful blast? He's Mr. Incredible, that's how, and I need him inside me.

Right fucking now.

He turns us around, so the water cascades over my chest while he clutches me to him from behind. His hands are everywhere, washing me clean from his seed. Rubbing my breasts. My pussy. His teeth nip sharply on my ear.

"Bend over," he whispers.

I obey without question. I can't stand to be without him one second more.

The water pounds along my back as I lean forward and press my palms against the wall. The rhythmic drumbeat adds to the sensation as he readies himself. He spreads my butt cheeks wide and the water trickles there too. It's warm and slippery as he sweeps the tip of his cock along my ass crack. Back and forth, he rubs himself over my sensitive sphincter, causing it to flex and tingle with pleasure, just like I did for him moments earlier. Maybe he's up for a little tit for tat.

I tense and look around at him. "Not my ass," I say. I'm no anal-play virgin, but right now, I'd rather feel him rubbing inside my core. "I want you in my pussy."

He cups my mound with his big hand and shakes his head. "Not here. Not yet."

Oh, fuck that domineering shit. I'm well past playing games. *"Why?"* I almost scream.

"You know what I am. What this cock can do. I'll shred a fucking condom." He jerks his palm against my pussy as if to emphasize his point. "I won't take the chance of you getting pregnant. Not until you're ready to decide our future, Astrid."

"But we've done it before," I whimper. Then suck in a sharp breath at the power emanating from him as he shakes his head again.

"That was when you believed birth control would protect you. When you believed you couldn't get pregnant. What do you believe now?"

"I…" I start, but the words trail off as I swallow hard.

I want to use my stand-by argument and say that I can't get pregnant. That even if I weren't taking quarterly shots to make certain, the miscarriage I had at sixteen made sure of it. I was so traumatized by the whole experience I've never wanted kids since.

I felt that little life inside me die. I don't ever want to go through that again. And that same sixth sense that tells me Casey's babies are growing fine, has always allowed me to be certain of one truth. That no matter how many times I fuck someone, I won't get pregnant if I don't want to.

But looking at his strong, virile body and feeling the answering need humming inside me, I no longer know what to believe. If he can manipulate the air I breathe, what else can he do?

Which brings us to another point. He spilled his super-sperm inside me at least a dozen times during that convention weekend. I've had my period since then, but still. What a stupid bullshit chance to take. "Do you mean to fucking tell me that I might have gotten *pregnant?*"

I straighten and try to move away from him, but all that does is help him pin me closer to his body, his cock wedged between my ass cheeks and his hand tight on my pussy. His other hand captures my jaw and pins my back against his hard chest. He holds my head steady as he whispers beside my ear. "I had control in Chicago, and more importantly, so did you. You believed your precious chemicals would protect you and they did. Belief is a powerful thing, Astrid. It channels our power. But controlling it is easier when we're far away from the north. It beats through us like a drumbeat here. Can't you feel it?"

"No," I snap. All I can feel is the racing of my heart and how much I want to fucking deck him. But pinned the way I am, the best I can do is jab my elbow into his ribs.

He doesn't even flinch. If anything, his hold on me tightens.

"You're full of doubt now," he murmurs beside my ear. "Until you've decided if you want my child, I'm fucking your sexy ass or nothing else."

"What kind of a fucked-up ultimatum is that?"

"A serious one."

There's an angry bite to his voice that makes me bristle. "Well here's my ultimatum. Let go of me, or so help me God, I'll scream."

"Yeah, you'll be screaming all right. You'll be begging me for more."

My protest is swallowed by his mouth as it covers mine. Firm, almost savage, he presses his lips down, hard. I try to move away, but his fingers anchor my jaw, keeping my head where he wants it so he can devour me.

I want to laugh, scream, push him away and at the same time pull him closer. The rational part of me struggles as panic shrieks in my veins to resist being ravaged. I'm stronger than this. I can take control. But an even wilder, more instinctual part rears its primal head and howls in savage glee. A howl that becomes a roar as his hand clasping my pussy gets to work.

Without warning, his fingers part my slit and slide up inside me. I freeze at the sudden intrusion, barely able to think, let alone move.

There is no hesitation in his touch. No gentle awakening. As his tongue penetrates my mouth, and his fingers my vagina, he simply takes possession of me.

Pulling me backward against him further, he bends his knees, adjusting his balance and making me lose mine. I spread my legs wide, seeking firm footing against the slippery, wet floor. And in that instant he pushes his fingers up deep, so very deep. Right into my core.

I gasp around his tongue.

He fills me completely. Stretches my tight channel, and then stretches it more as he adds another two fingers. Four inside. I think. Maybe more. Is he trying to fist me? It almost hurts, but I'm wet. Dripping inside. I like the pleasure and the bite of pain. It feels so good to give him control. I love his savage need, the one he can barely contain. It sets free the secret side of me, the part that wants him to punish me for defying him. For making him wait four fucking weeks to have me like this.

He fucks me hard and without mercy. With his fingers and his tongue.

His hand pumping fast. His lips bruising mine. His tongue fills my mouth like his cock did just a few minutes ago. Can he taste himself on me? Does he enjoy it as much as I do? I've never been into cocksucking much, but Race. Oh my God, *Race*.

I buck against his ass, feel his thick cock press along my crack. His fingers fuck me faster, and faster. The water cascades down my front, pebbling my nipples. The sound of the spray is broken by the wet slap and rhythmic suction of his fingers pumping within me. I'm tightening inside. It's too much too fast, almost sharp, but there's no way in hell I can stop it. No way in hell I want to.

My deep moan is a wail of pleasure and despair.

He rips his lips from mine, and the loss of his tongue inside my mouth is almost too much to bear. "Hush, baby," he murmurs by my ear. "I'll make it all better, I promise."

I whimper as I gasp for air. I need to steady myself. I reach back and clutch his hair. His hand moves from holding my jaw to pinning me across my chest instead.

"You're so fucking hot and wet," he says in his sexy, mesmerizing voice.

But his pounding is so intense. I'm stretched raw. One giant super-sensitive nerve ending that he's grinding. "Oh, fuck. Oh, oh, oh, oh—"

He pounds the words out of me in short little gasps. It's too much. Too fast. He's shredding me.

And I don't fucking care.

I clutch at him, and sag. The only thing holding up my jelly-like body is him. He's transformed me into a huffing, keening, trembling boneless doll. I am his plaything, and I want him to fucking play me hard.

Blood rushes through my veins, darkening my vision with a haze of red.

"I don't want to pass out. Oh God! I don't want to pass out again!" I plead.

"Do you want to come now?" he rasps beside my ear.

"Yes."

"Do I finger-fuck you good?"

"*Yes.*"

"Show me, baby. Show me how good."

I do as he says with a gush that, despite the streaming shower, drenches his hand and my thighs. My unintelligible scream of pleasure echoes loud in the small space, drowning out the pounding of the water. I clench and tremble, keeping his fingers locked inside me as the world spins fast.

"So beautiful," he murmurs tightening his arm around me. "Fucking gorgeous." Tremor after tremor wracks through me, soaking me with waves of bliss. God, it's so intensely good, I never want it to end.

"Nooo," I whimper as he slowly eases his fingers out of my swollen sheath. The loss is so strong I want to cry. I bury my face in his neck instead and inhale his wet alpine scent. It doesn't help. But at least the dampness rimming my eyes won't be seen. He broke open the emotions bottled inside of me just now, and the feeling is just too raw to contain.

"Ah, love," he murmurs into my hair as his fingers stroke the wet strands. "Come on, baby, let's get you dry."

As if from a distance, I hear the shower being turned off. But I'm limp. Too weak to move or stand. If he lets go of me I'll fall.

Scooping me up, he carries me back to the bedroom. I have a vague impression of being laid on the soft bed. Of warm, gentle towels drying me off and tying up my hair as I lie there, trying to remember what it feels like to breathe and think.

It's the slow gentle licks that bring me around. The lazy sweep of his tongue against my swollen, bruised pussy lips. It's such a change of tempo after his brutal near-fisting, it's almost too sweet to bear.

Lick.

His velvet tongue sweeps over my mound. Soft and gentle. His blue eyes watching me, warm pleasure banking their cobalt fire.

Lick.

He caresses my pussy, teasing the folds with his soft warm tongue, enjoying my taste with a lazy smile that matches mine.

A small part of me stirs, recognizing how good his licking feels. But what he's doing is so relaxing, it's more soothing than arousing. Cozy and soft. Not demanding. I could lie like this for hours, just drifting, with him settled comfortably between my legs, gently licking and the Northern Lights dancing on the ceiling.

Who the hell am I kidding? He's Race Lindstrom, and any moment now that thick cock of his will be penetrating me. He's hard and ready again, and still very much butt naked. His stamina is amazingly intense, and I can't deny I love how it makes me feel wild inside. He pushes every limit I've ever known. It's frightening and arousing at the same time, like a hook digging into my skin that's pleasurable despite the sting. But I'm certain it will cause real pain if it ever lets go.

I stir and gently touch his wet hair with my fingers. Despite being in a room made of ice and snow, he's warm and seems unaffected by any hint of cold. Then again, it doesn't feel nearly as cold as it did when I first arrived. Probably because he's set fire to my body and soul.

"I didn't pass out," I say, as if it's some sort of victory that I was able to hang onto reality for a change when he brought me to yet another mind-blowing orgasm. Which, on further reflection, it is. We're at about a thirty, seventy ratio of *petite mort*, for all the times he's brought me to orgasm since we met. And I have the feeling that number would be a lot higher except he holds himself back.

He smiles. "But you did scream."

"I told you I would."

"And I told you, you would, too." His eyes are bright as he teases me. "Now relax and enjoy my loving."

Loving. The word makes my skin prickle uncomfortably. "But don't you want to ass-fuck me?"

His brows arch so high I swear they nearly launch off his face. "Later," he says, his breath warm against my pussy. "We do have a party to go to."

I groan and clutch the covers as his licking moves dangerously close to my clit. "Like we'll ever get there if you keep on doing that."

"You taste so good, baby. I can't help it."

Lick.

"Mmmm," I say and settle deeper into the covers. "It does feel good. Are you sure we have to go to the party?"

A loud knock sounds on the door. I jerk upright as my heart skips a beat.

Race, however, doesn't even move, except to hold me still. His hands press against my thighs, keeping them spread wide while he continues his soft licking as if it's the sole purpose of his life.

"Astrid? Are you alive in there?" Casey's muffled voice sounds through the frosted glass door.

My fingers clutch Race's damp hair. He glances up at me from between my legs, looking slightly amused.

"Oh, God. It's Casey," I whisper. "I never called her back." But her timing...

Race shrugs. His fingers tighten on my thighs as he gives my clit a rough lick.

Stars burst in front of my eyes. I moan and fall back against the bed, my head hitting the pillow with a thump.

"Astrid?" Casey calls out again. The handle rattles and I can hear muffled voices speaking low and tense, as if concerned. "Answer me, sweetie. Are you okay?"

"I'm fine," I shout, my voice sounding hoarse and weak. Probably from screaming so much lately. "Just go away."

Race's eyebrows flick downward. "Astrid," he says in a scolding tone. "Is that any way to speak to your friends? Don't you want to invite them inside?"

"W-What?" I stammer. Then, as I read the intent in his eyes, I quickly add a harshly whispered, "*No!*" But my vigorous shake of my head and yank on his hair is ignored as Race glances at the door.

With a flick of his hand in the air, and a whispered word, the air inside the room stirs. At the same time, the latch pops open and the door swings inward, hitting the wall with a loud bang. A cold breeze whips into the room, along with the startled gazes of Casey and Lucas.

I gasp and roll sideways, trying to grab a blanket for coverage, but it's too late. They've seen Race, butt naked, lounging with his face between my legs. And me, lying butt-naked with his face between my legs. But mostly I'm certain they've seen his face between my legs.

And the arrogant grin on it.

The fucker.

"Well…" Casey says, a smile spreading across her lips. "Looks like you're not dead after all."

Chapter 6

"You are such a jerk. I still can't believe you did that. No wait. What am I saying? Of course you'd do it. You're a jerk," I say loudly so Race can hear me from the bathroom where I'm putting the finishing touches on my make-up. Staring into the mirror, I roll my eyes in exasperation as I finalize my mascara. Hair braided into twin pigtails. Valkyrie costume zipped up. In about ten seconds I'll be ready to kick some ass at this stupid Ice Hotel costume party. Starting with him.

"They liked what they saw," Race calls back from the bedroom, downplaying my feelings like he has for the past hour or so.

"It was embarrassing. You did it on purpose to humiliate me."

"I did it on purpose to prove a point."

"Which was?"

"That they liked what they saw."

"What the hell is that supposed to mean?" Is he implying that Casey and Lucas liked seeing us together as a couple, or seeing us together naked? Either way he's guaranteed I can never look them in the eye again without blushing. Then again, dressed the way I am right now, who's worried about blushing? I toss my mascara into my bag on the countertop and angrily stomp into the bedroom.

"You know what it means," he says as he turns to look at me. "You just don't—holy sweet fuck!" His eyes widen as he takes in my skin-tight costume, compete with winged helmet and conical bra cups. "Slay me now and take me to Valhalla, baby. You are one hot Valkyrie."

I stop mid-stride as I catch sight of him, my mind taking a header. Luckily I have a spear to lean on to prevent me from falling as all the blood in my body rushes to my clit with a dizzying sense of déjà vu.

We've been here before.

Four weeks ago at that fan expo convention, playing a game of dress-up. Last time I was Amazon Woman and he was Bat Guy. But somehow that Lycra superhero suit didn't fit him nearly as well as this costume does. Maybe it's the firm texture of the black neoprene thermal suit we've all been given to wear as a base to our costumes. But every delectable muscle on his body is outlined in vivid detail. From his powerful thighs and the cut of his tight hips to the heavy biceps. With his dark blond hair teased wild and his horned helmet on, he could be a Norse god in the flesh. A very sexy Norse god. Looking at me like I'm the best thing since all-day happy hour was declared in Valhalla.

"Hello, Thor," I say, managing to find my voice. "Love your big hammer."

He grins and tosses the oversized prop he's holding onto the bed. "I know you do, baby." I'd take offence to his arrogant tone, except that yeah, it's true. He wields Mjolnir like a god, inside and outside of bed.

He moves closer and circles me, raking me with his intense gaze.

"No panty line," he murmurs, admiring my ass and smoothing his hand over the curve-hugging fabric. "Are you bare under there, sweetheart?"

A shiver wracks me as the powerful I'm-in-control aura emanating from him fuels my already searing desires. I give a little shrug to cover it up and try for nonchalant. "Maybe I am, maybe I'm not."

Moving to stand in front of me, he taps the hard plastic cups molded over my breasts. The hunger in his eyes burns bright as he plays with the sculpted tips and smiles that wicked, knowing smile of his. "Maybe I should toss you over my shoulder and find out now." Sweeping his long, Viking cloak over his shoulder, he bends onto one knee to get a better look at the other piece of armor I have on: a pair of silver and gold bikini-style bottoms sewn over the top of my bodysuit like a chastity belt. "This is nice," he says. Using his finger, he follows the line of plastic chain-mail fabric where it passes between my legs. "But completely unnecessary."

"Race," I groan through gritted teeth, trying hard not to show my pussy-throbbing reaction to his touch. "I'm still really pissed with you."

He looks up at me, the heat in his gaze a palpable thing. "You look beautiful, Astrid," he says in a soft, silky tone that does interesting things to my insides and tries to dampen my annoyance. But still, I'm not buying it. I'm quite familiar with his game.

"Flattery will get you intimate with the tip of my spear," I growl in warning.

His brows flick. "Ouch," he says as he straightens to his full six foot four height, forcing me to look up at him again. "Don't tease me like that, baby."

Hand on hip, I match his imposing stance as I glance the full length of his impressive body. I let my gaze linger on the heavy erection bulging from beneath his Viking-style tunic, and then trail back up to meet his eyes again. "Who says I'm teasing?"

He laughs and grabs my spear from me. "Let's get rid of the weaponry, shall we?" He tosses it onto the bed beside his plastic hammer and wraps his arm around my shoulders. "I have a much better thing for you to wear with your costume."

"I'm serious, Race," I say, trying to shake his hold on me by pushing him aside. But he's not letting go, and neither is his sexy scent. It fills my nostrils, the hint of pine reminding me of that orgasm he gave me in the woods. Ha, like I could ever forget that experience. I shake my head to clear it. "I'm still angry," I insist but the heat in my voice sounds like it's fading, even to me. "You can't just do shit to people and think it's okay."

"I know," he says and drags me over to the dresser. "You're right. Choice is very important," he adds. "Which is why I want you to wear these tonight." He picks up the golden bracelets he gifted me with earlier. Cupping them in his large hand, he holds them out to me to take. "Beautiful jewelry for my exquisite Valkyrie."

I stare at them glinting softly in the light, my stomach twisting with a resurgence of anxiety. "Oh, hell no. No, no. No." I've been ignoring them since opening that box, hoping he'd forget they existed. Or make them go *poof*, like my clothes.

His smile slips from his lips even as his grip on my shoulders tightens. "What do you mean, no?"

Ah, hell. "Look, Race. They're very nice. But I don't want them." I haven't opened any of the gifts he's ever sent me. I haven't wanted to encourage him. But maybe it's been mostly out of the fear of losing myself to him even more than I already have. "I didn't open the box. Casey did. Why don't you give them to her instead?"

He stares at me nonplussed. "Because I didn't make them for her. I made them for you."

"I never asked you to."

His arm slips from my shoulders. He leans sideways against the dresser, his cobalt eyes turning to flinty steel. "It wouldn't be much of a gift if you had. Did you read the inscription?"

"What?" I stare at him blankly, my mind trying to register why he looks so upset, and why I should care.

"Did you read…the inscription?" he repeats, his voice a mockery of patience.

"Um…no."

His lips press into a thin line as he holds the bracelets out to me again and waits for me to take them.

I do so, hesitantly, unimpressed with the mix of anger and hurt billowing off him in waves. What the hell do I have to feel guilty for? If he's bought me something, then fine. But it's not much of a gift if I'm just supposed to accept it without question. I don't want that kind of obligation in my life.

I turn the bracelets around, examining the beautifully crafted surface of smooth gold, and the inner midnight-blue velvet lining. There, along the inside edge where the lining meets the hinge on the left bracelet.

The choice…is inscribed.

And on the same place on the right one…*will always be yours.*

I glance sharply at him and catch the storm brewing within his eyes. The air in the room is heavy. I can't tell if it's him or me, but I find it hard to breathe as I trace the incised letters with my fingers. The metal is cool to my touch, but I'm suddenly hot as I speak the words out loud. "The choice will always be yours."

A thousand ideas flash through my mind of what that phrase could mean, but one stands out. He's said those same words to me before, the first time we spent the night together. When he held my wrists over my head, plastic Amazon Woman bracelets gripped tight against my skin. His devotion imprinted on me through his taste, scent and words.

"I can take the blindfold off whenever I want to?"

"Of course. The choice will always be yours."

I trusted him, then.

To keep me safe as we made love. To fill me with his passion and make the lonely places inside me disappear. To fuck me senseless and never let go until I was good and ready.

But he hasn't ever let go.

Because deep inside, I've never been ready to let him.

Despite my anger over his deception, I've kept the connection alive. I could have blocked his number on my phone. Told Casey I wouldn't come on this trip or be part of any stupid promotional crap with him. If I'd really wanted to never see him again, I could have cut all ties.

But I haven't, and I didn't, and he knows it. These bracelets I'm holding in my shaking hands are a reminder of his commitment to me that the choice *has* always been mine.

So I should be firm with him now, right? Stop this thing in its tracks. Tell him to take back the bracelets and leave me the hell alone forever. But for the life of me, as I stand here struggling to breathe with my heart squeezing tight and my pulse thundering in my ears, I can't.

I can't ignore the fact that regardless of his superhuman ability in pissing me off, the connection between us is hooked deep inside me. He got under my skin before I had a chance to walk away with no regrets. And that's the worst thing about all this. I would regret leaving him now. He's an ass, but he's my ass, and I would always wonder if we couldn't make it work. That, and the uncomfortable truth that being apart from him hurts.

It physically fucking hurts.

Like a piece of my soul is missing. I only feel complete when he's around. The last four weeks of tortured sleep have shown me that.

He swallows hard, his gaze never wavering from mine. "The choice will always be yours, Astrid. The choice to stay. The choice to leave. I will never hold you against your will." His hand lifts to caress my cheek.

I curl toward him as the deepest part of me responds. But his gloved fingers barely brush my skin before they clench into a fist that drops to his side. His gorgeous face sets in hard lines, the agony etched there very real.

And I can't shake the feeling that there is more meaning to him in this gift of choice than there is for me.

He may have deceived me at times, but he's never crossed that one line. Whatever his own desires, he's respected my choice. Even in the shower and his raging need, he didn't ass-fuck me when I said no. He hasn't done anything to me, if I've said no and truly meant it.

But maybe he hasn't always done so with others.

The rawness haunting his stare is like a clamp squeezing my insides as apprehension trickles through my veins. But I don't look away. I can't. I have to know.

"Why does it matter so much, Race?"

His jaw is so hard it could crack. He takes a deep breath as he studies me. Then another. "I never want you to feel…chained." He nods, a small, sharp movement that is almost a flinch, acknowledging the deeper question I'm asking. "I was married once. But I think you know that already?"

I match his sharp nod with one of my own as my heart misses a beat. "I Googled you after we met," I admit, not liking where this conversation is going.

Amongst the articles about his business successes and a few pics of him attending various functions with a different woman at his side each time, the notation about his brief marriage stood out. I'd be lying if I said I wasn't curious about the woman who'd captured his heart. Or the pang of jealousy that speared me when I thought of her and Race sharing a life. Or the fact that jealousy is even sharper as we talk about her now. "I'm sorry for your loss," I offer as condolence. "It must have been very hard when she died."

Charity Lindstrom was a pretty woman, tall and slender with beautiful, dark almond-shaped eyes. According to her obituary from ten years ago, she was loved and missed by her family. And judging by the deep sadness etched in Race's entire being, loved and missed by her husband, too.

Grief for him curls in my chest and gives my lungs a hard kick, and for a moment all I can do is stare at him while the world narrows into a tight wedge of pain.

"Yes," he says, his gaze never wavering from mine. "We were married about two years when she took her own life."

"Oh, God…" Her obituary never said that, but of course it wouldn't. Who would want that legacy to be printed for the world to see?

He grimaces, cutting off my strangled cry. "I thought if I tried hard enough, I could make it work for both of us. I thought if I could make her happy, then everything would be fine." He sucks in a sharp breath, the flash of pain in his eyes undisguised. "I was wrong."

I think of his magnificent power, and how careful he is to hide it. The struggle he must have faced to make sense of it all while growing up. And the troubled man that he is, standing before me now. Lonely and alone. When it comes to love, apparently even a demigod can't always get what he wants. But the strength and vulnerability that fills him makes him more real than anyone I've ever known.

"I'm so sorry," I whisper again. I stare at the bracelets clutched in my hands, my heart and mind spinning.

I know what it is to have loved and lost, the empty ache forever throbbing inside. Time doesn't heal wounds, it just numbs them. But right now I'm bleeding with shame as I remember my cruel words on the plane.

Do you even know what love is, Race?

I'd thought him an arrogant bastard unaffected by the world around him. But now I'm wondering if it isn't the reverse. That he feels it all too deeply, like me, and tries to control it in order to stay sane.

Damn him.

I don't want to deal with his shit. I can barely deal with my own. He's a manipulative ass, but a gorgeous one. Powerful and sensitive all at once.

But I'm not going to walk this path blindly. Not this time. This time I need more.

"What happened? What aren't you telling me, Race?" The words slip softly off my lips, loud in the silence of the room.

The despair storming within him wraps around him, veiling his eyes as he glances at the bracelets in my hands. "I found out who I really am," he whispers.

A shiver wracks me as the air turns cold. "What does that mean?"

He studies me, his eyes like raw wounds. "It will be easier if I show you."

I shake my head, frustration to know what the big deal is making me irritated. "Show me what? You can't just level me with something like that and then back off."

"My life. My mistakes. My reality." He pauses, and the veil lifts for a brief moment. But the mixture of helplessness and hope within him is almost too much to witness. "My home."

"Your home?"

He nods. "My house. It's…not something I show most people. But I'll take you there tomorrow. If you'd like."

The world tilts slightly as I suck in air. "Oh, my God. Do you mean to tell me you have a, a…*fortress of solitude?*"

A smile cracks his lips. "Ah, hell, Astrid. You blow me away." He shakes his head, the sadness easing within him as laughter builds inside. "You're the only person in the world who'd think of *Superman* at a time like this." His gaze becomes soft a second before he leans forward and places a gentle kiss upon my forehead.

The tenderness in that touch makes me almost want to cry, but I push away the feeling and grasp at something lighter instead. "Why not?" I shrug, wondering why I'm even surprised by anything anymore. I mean, we're standing here talking about his tragic past while dressed up as characters from Norse mythology. Except he, at least, isn't really a myth. "Makes sense to me," I explain. "You're some kind of superhero-god-person, right? Of course you'd have a freakin' fortress of solitude to hide your secrets in."

He laughs and his gorgeous eyes brighten. "You've been hanging out at Comic Conventions with Casey too much. It's my family's home. They've lived there for generations."

"Who lives there now?"

He grimaces. "Ghosts. Memories. Take your pick."

I feel my eyes widen. If anyone else had said that, I'd think they were being metaphorical. But I've known him long enough to understand there's a hidden truth in everything he says. Especially the most impossible sounding things. And I really, really hope he doesn't mean his dead wife is haunting him for real, but that's probably just what he means, isn't it?

I swallow hard. "Well, shit."

"Yeah."

My heart is pounding a million drumbeats a minute. I don't want to see the vulnerable look in his eyes, the naked loneliness tinged with regret and pain, but I can't look away now. Any more than I could look away when I first saw him walking toward me across that crowded convention room in Chicago.

Don't do it, don't do it, don't do it.

This whole situation screams at me to run and hide. Just fuck him and leave him, and not get emotionally involved. But the bottom line is, I've spent the last month trying to avoid the truth. It's too late. I am emotionally involved. I could pretend I don't care, but it would be a lie. His grief calls to me as deeply as mine. It bothers me to see him haunted. And I've never been afraid of ghosts, real or otherwise.

"Okay," I say, feeling a bit like I'm jumping off a bridge to my doom, but the plunge is exciting rather than scary. "I'd like to see your home and its…secrets. But under one condition."

"What's that?"

"You wear the bracelets."

His brows flick. "They won't fit. They were made for your exquisitely slender wrists, my goddess." He picks up my hand and holds it against his large one as if to emphasize his point.

"You're a guy who makes clothes go *poof* and you can't make some bracelets grow bigger to fit you?" I taunt.

He stares at me for a full, long minute. "Are you sure this is what you want?"

"Yes."

"All right. But if I do this, you're going to let me fuck you any way, any how and as often as I want tonight. I need to feel your bliss, sweetheart. It's the only thing that makes sense in my life."

"Um…" I say as my core instantly tingles at his hot words and the need reverberating in them. My traitorous nipples tighten, little wanton buds of desire, begging for his lips. "Whatever happened to it being my choice?"

But the decision is made before I even get the words out of my mouth. He takes the bracelets from my hand and presses them around his wrists. The air stirs as energy passes from him into the metal, expanding and smoothing it into a pair of bracers that go perfectly with his own costume. In fact, they seem to make his arms even more impressively, massively god-like. His Thor cloak flutters slightly as the air stirs again.

"Now," he says catching my gaze with a look full of hot promise, "the choice is mine. And I choose you, Astrid. All of you. Forever."

"Ah…" I manage past the sudden lump in my throat. What the hell just happened? I shake my head, not wanting to even think about it. All I know is that despite standing in a room made of snow, it's freaking hot in the suit I'm wearing. And being so near him and the sexy heat he exudes isn't doing anything to cool things down. Grabbing my gloves from the bed, I fan them in front of me. "You know what? I think I need a stiff drink. I'll see you at the party."

He grins and holds his hand out toward the door. With a stirring of air, it opens wide. "After you, my gorgeous Valkyrie."

Leaving my spear behind, I head for the bar, Race two steps behind. But I have the unnerving feeling that he's really been two steps ahead of me all the way.

***

"Okay," Casey says as she raises her goblet of ginger ale to my Sex on The Beach. They meet with a solid *thunk* rather than a *clink*. But I guess that's to be expected with tumblers carved from blocks of pure, crystal-clear ice. "To a weekend full of amazing friends and even more amazing sex," she toasts, in a tone loud enough to be heard above the steady beat of music throbbing through the air. Then she takes a sip and pins me with her most pinning stare. "Now. What the hell is going on between you and Race?"

I pause before taking a sip of the crisp, cool liquid, then down half the tumbler in one go. "I don't know," I gasp, setting the drink down on our small table near the dance floor. The alcohol burns as much as it numbs, but nothing can ever drown out the steady presence of Race Lindstrom.

"You don't know?"

"Nope."

She grins and leans on her elbows towards me across the table. "Well, judging by the way he keeps staring at you like he wants to eat you alive, I'd say things are happening on the bed, on the floor, in the shower…" She breaks off, giggling.

I give her a playful swat and join in the giggles. "You had to go there, didn't you?"

"Oh, hell yeah." She raises a speculative brow as she glances past me again at Race, where he's lounging by the bar itself, speaking with Lucas. The soft blue lights embedded into the blocks of ice that make up the bar shine onto both of them. The glow outlines their fit bodies and doesn't leave much to the imagination. "He's really, um, built, isn't he?"

"Yep. And I'll ask you to keep your eyes on your own super-sexy man beast, thank you very much."

"Oh, my God. You're jealous!" She puts down her drink and covers her mouth with her fingers, trying unsuccessfully to stop her excited laughter.

"I am not," I say. But before we can end up in another epic *no-I'm-not, yes-you-are* battle, I change the subject. "What do you think they're talking about?" Whatever it is, it involves a heavy amount of narrowed looks, intense conversation and glances our way.

"You. Lucas is giving him a man-talk."

I snort and roll my eyes. "Oh, yeah. I can just imagine. 'Hey bro, did you get it in there yet?' 'Hell, yeah. So how about those Packers?'"

Casey shakes her head, making the ears on her Steam Bunny costume wiggle. "He's just making sure Race is on the straight with you, and what will happen to him if he isn't."

Warmth fills my heart at how my BFF and her man want to look out for me, but really, I can't imagine there's anything Lucas can physically do to a guy who can make the weather change with the flick of his hand. "Thanks, but it's all good," I say, hoping it's the truth.

The only thing I'm certain of is how my heart pounds when I think of the impending sex-a-thon Race has in mind tonight before taking me to his mysterious fortress of solitude tomorrow and the deep dark secrets it hides. And I can't decide if I should head back to our room now and get naked or order another drink.

"Really?" Her eyes flash with annoyance. "Because you've been a bit psycho lately. And I'd really like my happy BFF back."

"I'm sorry," I say and mean it from the bottom of my heart. "It's just…I don't know what to think anymore. Race is so different from anyone I've ever met." I almost laugh at the understatement, but plunge on instead, keeping my gaze glued to hers. "He makes me nuts. On one hand he's this gorgeous guy who really seems to care. And on the other he just wants what he wants, you know? He's so in control all the time. I don't know if I should kiss him or kick his ass."

A smile pulls at her lips as she studies me. "He's a guy," she says. "Driving women nuts is their superpower. I can't tell you how many times I've felt like kicking Lucas in the ass for one reason or another. But kissing is a much more effective way of resolving our differences."

I snicker and glance over my shoulder at the guys again, thinking of Race's true superpower. My man can work the weather and make love to me until I pass out from the bliss, without him even breaking a sweat. And he looks damn hot dressed as a Viking god. Strong. Powerful. Each muscle a temptation I'm hard pressed to resist.

His gaze catches mine. The flash of hunger in his eyes is so strong it makes my sex clench with need. For a moment, all I can do is stare back and share his secret little smile, while trying to remember to breathe.

"You're really okay, Astrid?"

Casey's question makes me blink. "Yes," I say automatically. "Well, sort of," I add as I look at her and shake my head, trying to clear it of the dizzying attraction I have for Race. I'm torn between feeling slightly nauseous over the idea of trusting him with any kind of real relationship and wanting this party to be done so I can get him alone and fuck him senseless for a change. "I just...I can't stop thinking about him."

"Sweetie," Casey says, "You haven't stopped thinking about him since you first saw him at the convention. You two can't keep your eyes off each other. Maybe you should give him a chance and see where it takes you?"

"And if it takes me straight to a broken heart again?"

She leans back on her chair, considering me. "I was like that with Lucas, you know. So sure he would break my heart that I ended up making it happen. But he wasn't the bad guy. It was me. I wanted him to fuck up so that I had a reason to leave." She glances at her drink and twists it around on the table for a second, but I see the pain lurking in her eyes.

The memories are still sharp, of how things were uncertain for her and Lucas just four weeks ago. I remember her tears all too well. Her insecurities and the pain she and Lucas went through. I was there. Helping her cope with it all. Just like she's doing with me.

Her lips twist into a little smile as her gaze finds mine again. "Loving someone means trusting them. It was the hardest thing I've ever done, learning to accept life has no guarantees. But I love him so much, in the end the decision was easy. Do you think I made a bad choice?"

"No."

"Then what are you waiting for?"

"Race is different."

"Yeah?" she says as she flicks her gaze around the room. "He's different, all right. Different than what I expected from the media slings and rumors. I can't say what kind of person he's been in the past, but he's the most down-to-earth rich guy I've ever met."

She cuts off my indrawn breath with a wave of her hand. "I'm not saying he's perfect. I know he's been an ass sometimes. But just look at this place. It's so beautiful. The lights, the music. I can't wait to see the chapel tomorrow and start planning the wedding for next year. It's going to be so special for Lucas. And it's all because of Race. This party, the show, the costumes, everything. He's made it all happen for us."

"I doubt he'd do it if it wasn't good business for him," I point out.

"Of course," she agrees, "but look at him." She nods her head toward the bar where Race is still speaking with Lucas, a slight scowl on his face. "He'll probably make a mint off this whole deal, but he didn't have to come in person, you know." Her gaze roams around the packed room, taking in the crowd. "All these people want a piece of him. But who's he been spending most of his time with? You. That seems like a guy with his priorities in the right place to me."

"Why are you trying so hard to sell him on me?"

Her lips pull into a pout. "I just want to see you happy."

"And you think he's the man for the job, even after the shit he pulled at the convention?"

She shakes her head and takes a sip of her ginger ale. "No one can make you happy except you, Astrid. But it's a little bit easier to make that choice if you're with someone who puts a smile on your face. And you two… The way you're looking at each other tonight. You're supercalifragilisticexpialidocious-sized smiling."

"Fan-fucking-tastic," I mutter and down the rest of my drink. "My BFF's freakin' Mary Poppins."

"Sweetie." She laughs. "Mary Poppins didn't ever wear a costume as tight as this." She strikes a pose, showing off her Victorian-style Steam Bunny outfit that makes her boobs stick out like grenades. They are awkwardly hard to miss staring at, but that's the way she likes it.

I giggle and glance aside as her hand tightens on mine, her gaze trained on something off to the left. "Ah, hell. That stupid camera crew is coming our way again."

"Yeah. Need I remind you this was your idea in the first place? Let's just go hide in the bathroom or something." Actually, maybe it's the buzz from the booze, but I'm ready to head back to my room and see just how big of a Mary Poppins-sized smile Race can put on my face.

"Hide? Dressed like this?" She laughs and threads her fingers through mine before I can pull away. "No freaking way. It's time to show those chicken-shit guys of ours what we're made of. We're going dancing, Astrid. And we're gonna own it."

Chapter 7

"Jesus fucking Christ," Lucas Haskell says. He sets his drink on the bar with a *thunk*, his gaze never wavering from the two women dancing at the center of our universe. "Are you seeing this?"

"Hell, yeah," I say. Like I could look at anything else. Astrid moves like liquid sex. All sensual and sleek with a smile that's brighter than a thousand suns when she laughs. It burns my heart as she looks at me, singeing me with her desire. I'll likely get incinerated by the end of tonight, but my gods, what a way to go.

I take a sip of my water. It slides down cold, but does nothing to relieve the heat flaring inside me, urging me to end this party and fuck her six ways to Sunday while I still can. 'Cause after tomorrow, there's no way in hell she'll let me anywhere near her again.

Casey does a little sultry wiggle, making her Steam Bunny tail flutter as she turns and beckons for Lucas to join her, dancing in front of the camera recording her every movement.

He groans and shakes his head. "Do you see what I mean now?" he asks me.

"Hey, man," I say, "you wanted this wedding show to happen."

"No. *She* wanted the show. I just wanted to get married."

"So? Go marry her then. I'll have the chapel set up for you tomorrow."

"Can't," he says and his jaw tightens. "She wants to wait until the kids are born. She wants them to be there, too, for the pictures."

Not for the first time I feel a pang of envy over the life this man has. A normal life, with a woman who loves him. And twins on the way. Kids, the most precious gift of all. What I wouldn't give to have a chance at even half that. I know how easy it can all be taken away. "Shit," I say and manage a smile. "She kinda has you by the balls there."

"Yeah. She's great at giving them a squeeze."

I laugh, despite the ache threatening to twist inside me. "I can see why she and Astrid are best friends."

"Dude," Lucas says, with a chuckle. "You'll have better luck with Astrid if you stop standing here with your dick in your hands. Go show her you mean business."

I take another sip of my drink and glance at him, amused by how he's tossing back at me the same advice I just gave him. He's dressed like a Victorian gentleman, complete with top hat, and looks every inch the part. But I understand the solid streak of risk-taking wildness that exists within him. He's a child of Minerva and Bacchus, though I've never seen him lose control with drink. Just like his Casey is a true Muse blessed by Aphrodite and has the charismatic allure to show for it.

"Easier said than done," I say. Despite the impatience pumping through my veins to bury my cock balls-deep inside Astrid, I want her to come to me this time. I want to see the choice she's making clear in her eyes and smile. Not these little coy looks she tosses my way, tempting me to say fuck it and just fuck her. I want this night to be special for her. As special as I can make it.

Lucas cocks his brow as he nods towards where the girls are doing an impromptu version of the Macarena. "See that red-haired beauty dressed as a Victorian sex-bomb? She's the love of my life. My reason for breathing. She calls the shots when we're in the office. But in the bedroom, she likes it when I'm in charge."

"Keep her fucked, keep her happy. Is that it?"

His cocky smile slips. "Look man, I almost lost Casey. No way in hell am I ever going through that again. I had blue balls for three fucking weeks. I practically ripped my dick off just thinking of her. But I waited too long to make my move. Gave her time to think of all kinds of crazy ideas about why we couldn't get married. Take it from me, you need to go over there and sort your shit out with Astrid. Right now."

"It's complicated," I say. My pulse spikes as I think of how things will be tomorrow once I've introduced her to the true hell that is my life. How quickly will the sexy smile leave her eyes when she sees what I've done?

Haskell shakes his head. "No, seriously," he says. "You need to sort out your shit with her. All this drama is upsetting Casey. And I can't have her upset."

I smile despite the anxiety biting at me. His claim on Casey is indisputable. A lesser man might be jealous of all the attention she attracts. She's sinuous, graceful, as she moves her hips, her breasts jiggling to the beat, daring everyone in the room not to watch. She loves the attention, her smile bright as people clap and whistle their appreciation.

But Haskell ignores them, and I can see why as she glances our way again. She only ever has eyes for him, and the look in them glows with pleasure. It's clear she enjoys being in the spotlight, but she does it all for him. And that devotion is mirrored in him.

Love.

I caught a glimpse of that once with Astrid, after the first time we had sex. With the warmth of her cradled against my body, and my heart beating in tune with hers. The spark of recognition filled her eyes as she looked at me and smiled.

Is it too much to want that again?

Maybe.

Maybe that kind of love isn't written in the stars for me.

But I have to think that, as she looks at me now with a seductive smile and a sassy flick of her Valkyrie braids, as she begs me to come to her with a sexy crook of her finger that grabs me deep inside, there's a glimmer of hope.

"Enough," I say. "It's time." I put my tumbler onto the bar and concentrate on her desire.

Haskell grins at me and lifts his own tumbler with a quick nod. "Good luck, dude." He downs the remainder of his drink in one gulp.

But he doesn't really understand. "You might want to get Casey to your room now," I warn. "Because this party is about to get a hell of a lot hotter." Already the mood in the room is shifting, becoming more seductive. It's gaining energy from Astrid as she works her body on the dance floor, the music pulsing through her like a drum beat.

My goddess likes to watch people fucking.

She gets off on the sights and sounds of sex, and I want her to have everything she's ever desired tonight. She deserves all the complete and utter bliss I can give her.

But I'm not so keen on the idea of it being filmed. Catching the eye of the lead cameraman I silently instruct, *leave*. The response is instantaneous. As if thinking of the idea themselves, the three men turn off their equipment and head for the exit. Casey stares after them, looking slightly bemused. But with a shrug of her shoulders, she continues dancing, her eyes hot for Lucas.

"Yeah, leave and miss all the fun?" Haskell says, abandoning his empty glass on the bar. His brow furrows a bit as he glances about the room, picking up on the change in mood. The way people are dancing closer, brushing against each other with their bodies and mouths. "Good luck with that idea. You have met my fiancée, haven't you?"

I laugh as we head toward our women. If something sexy is going on, Casey will want to be in the middle of it. But I really don't care about Haskell's issues, because Astrid is glowing softly as she sways to the music.

Literally glowing.

The lights pick up the metallic decoration on her suit, but it's more the sexy confidence shining from her smile. Not for the first time, I wonder how anyone could miss the goddess she is inside. There's beauty and then there's Astrid—the most sensual woman

I've ever met in my life. She's tall and lithe, the opposite of Casey, with her small breasts and long, slender fuck-me legs. Eyes closed, she twines her arms above her head in a sinuous dance of seduction that beckons me to join her. No way in hell can I ever walk away from her. I'd rather die.

As the gyrating crowd parts to let me through, I can't help speculating how many children she will unwittingly cause to be conceived tonight, with desire shining from her so bright and the power of the Aurora beating through her veins. She doesn't understand the influence she wields in this world.

My cock is hard, pressing against my tight suit as I reach her.

"Du är utsökt, vet du det? Gud, jag vill knulla dig så hårt," I murmur beside her ear as I wrap my arms about her waist.

She shudders, a delicious shiver of pleasure, as I pull her backward against my chest. Her eyes flash open. "Race! I love it when you speak Swedish. What did you say?"

I don't bother with a literal translation. "I can't wait anymore, Astrid. I need you, baby. Now."

She turns in my arms. Her lips whisper across my cheek before her hot breath caresses my ear. "I think I want that, too."

Her vulnerable, almost hesitant, words are fire in my veins. My heart skips a beat, but the rest of me becomes liquid heat at the sexy sound of her need for me. Her arms slip around my chest as she moves restlessly against me, trailing wet kisses down my neck.

I move my hands from her hips and smooth them upward along her back, enjoying the feel of her slight curves and the pressure as the hard shells covering her breasts crush against my chest.

Her palm caresses my nape a second before her fingers grasp my Viking helmet and she tosses it away into the crowd. A teasing smile twists her lips as her fingers spear into my hair, ruffling it. Her eyes light up, burning with the same fire that fills me.

Fucking hell. I shudder inside at that hungry look. Maybe outward too, at her indrawn breath and the way it brushes against my skin.

I grasp her Valkyrie hat by the wings and send it soaring into the crowd too.

She glances sideways, following the arc, and seems startled, as if remembering we're in a packed room. But the dancers around us are more interested in each other as they enjoy the heavy beat of the music. Swaying, kissing. Groping. Dry fucking.

"Whoa," she says, her eyes growing wide.

It doesn't seem to matter who is with whom. A blond Adonis dressed as Hercules is slow-grinding his girlfriend's ass, while another guy joins in. A couple of nearby girls are fondling each other where they sway, lip-locked on the dance floor.

Casey and Lucas are making out hard in front of us. They slowly stagger and crash through the jumble of bodies. Maybe heading toward the exit and their room. Maybe just to the nearest fuck-me surface. Casey, at least, has never been shy.

Astrid's erotic energy fills the room, burning me, tempting me to strip down and fuck her right here. Maybe she would like it amongst the naked limbs, jostling and flailing as costumes are abandoned. A sexy groan comes from a threesome crashing onto a fur rug on the floor nearby.

It should be cold, but it's not. I've heated things to well above the -5C needed to keep the icy walls from melting. But I've protected them, too, with a thin bubble of air. I don't want the place collapsing and anyone getting hurt.

Astrid sways in my arms, consumed by the energy swirling around us, her chest heaving, her body shaking with her growing need. Maybe it's too much. Maybe too obvious a distraction, but I want to give her everything. All the pleasure she's ever desired and more.

When the sun rises, I'll deal with tomorrow. And the prospect has me bleeding inside. Showing Astrid that side of me, the deepest darkest most vulnerable side…I might as well run a hot poker through my heart, because her rejection will feel the same.

I shouldn't have brought her here. I should have stayed away. But it's the right thing to do, letting her know the full truth, even if it means things will change after tonight. But how can I ever let her go? Her warmth is the only thing that eases the ache inside.

Maybe that's why I clutch her so tight and want to fuck her so hard tonight. I want to give her enough pleasure to last us a hundred lifetimes.

She can't seem to look away from the entwined bodies dancing and swaying around us. Arousal floods her veins, pounding through her and into me as she gyrates her hips in time with mine.

"Race," she hisses, her gloved fingers catching in my hair. Her pupils are wide, dilated, her breath uneven. "What is going on? Are you doing this?"

I nod in answer, but it really isn't me. She's the one who likes to watch. I'm just channeling her desires into the air for everyone to breathe.

She blinks and shakes her head as if trying to clear it. "You have to stop."

"Why? I want to give you the world, Astrid."

"It isn't right," she insists. "Making people do this."

I smile reassuringly. "I'm not making them do anything. All I do is give a suggestion. If they didn't really want to do this deep down inside, they would leave."

"But Casey and Lucas—" She looks around in a panic for her friends.

"Are over there, having the time of their life. It's fine," I insist. I nod toward an alcove of seats where they're enjoying each other's company on a pile of reindeer furs.

Her mouth drops open. But still she resists. "I…okay, but…"

"Is it too much for you, baby? Would you rather be more private?" There's a big difference between seeing and being seen.

She nods.

I weave a path through the clinging bodies to the alcove near Casey and Lucas. A frosted partition of ice separates our seats from theirs and the rest of the room, giving us the ability to observe more quietly. Grabbing a stack of furs of my own for added comfort, I settle Astrid on my lap and fit her snug against me.

"Hide," I say and a wave of my hand makes the air before us thicken into a semi-transparent wall. It dims the moans of pleasure and turns the sights of writhing bodies into a blur. Not that anyone would notice us anyway in the mood they are in.

"Now," I say as I nuzzle her cheek. I remove her gloves, and toss them to the ground. "You don't need to worry about the others. They won't do anything they don't want to do or remember anything tomorrow. It'll all be a blur. Just a wicked dream."

"I like the wicked part," she says with a smile in her voice. But she's tense in my arms, squirming and restless.

I nibble lightly on her ear as I brush my fingers along her thighs. Her gaze is glued to the scene beside us through the hazy pane of ice. There's enough distinction to make out shapes. Lucas is on his knees, leaning forward to caress Casey's body while she lies before him on the furs.

"They're so beautiful together," Astrid murmurs. "You can tell how much he loves her with every touch."

Is that what she wants tonight? Not the orgy I've given her?

Chuckling inside, I shift us slightly to watch her friends more easily. Astrid's ass rubs my cock as she settles against me again. I'm hard as hell, but she's more pliant now, less tense. Her body charges with excitement as I brush one hand over her hip and across her thighs.

I press my other palm against the hard wall of ice. The heat of my hand makes the frosted centre become clearer in a spiraling pattern that spreads outward.

Astrid sucks in a sharp breath as Casey and Lucas's bodies become visible through the barrier.

"Can they see us now too?"

"If they come up from air long enough to notice. Stop fussing and enjoy the show. You know they love it." *And so do you.*

She giggles, and the sound of her pleasure is like music to my ears.

It's clear by Casey's movements that she wants something fast and urgent, but Lucas is being gentle with her. Taking his time, making certain she's safe as he slowly removes her clothing.

Astrid's breathing hitches as Casey's full breasts appear. Lucas strokes them lovingly, his thumbs teasing her taut nipples, his eyes never leaving her face as he gauges how much pressure to use.

Casey arches her back, her eyes shut and her lips parted as she enjoys the feeling of his hands stroking and kneading her flesh.

"Oh, my God," Astrid whispers as a deep blush stains her cheeks. "I really shouldn't be watching this." But she's unable to look away. I know deep down inside she doesn't want to.

I slide my hands up Astrid's tight belly to fondle her breasts, but the plastic shells of her Valkyrie costume are in the way.

"We don't really need clothes, do we?" I murmur by her ear. I touch the zipper of her costume and it instantly peels away, exposing her flawless skin to my greedy eyes.

She lets out a soft gasp of surprise that quickly turns to a grin as all of our clothing disappears with a snap of my fingers.

"*Poof,*" she says and rubs her bare back against my chest, enjoying the feel of my hairs as they tickle her skin and the way my stiff cock twitches against her ass crack. "I love how you do that."

"Mmm." I nibble her earlobe. "What else do you love? Something stiff and long, perhaps? Filling you in here?" I caress her smooth sex with my fingers.

She jerks slightly and sucks her bottom lip between her teeth with a soft gasp. Her gaze is filled with raw need as she watches the scene through the ice, the moans of pleasure from the orgy around us filtering through the barrier.

Lucas has his pants off and his cock out. Casey's eyes are riveted to the sight of him as he thrusts himself back and forth between her breasts. His face is set in a rictus of pleasure. It won't be long before he's blowing his load all over her voluptuous body. The sight of them together is interesting to watch, but I'm more excited by what it's doing to Astrid.

She's squirming in my lap, all hot and sexy and driving me wild, her honey-warm scent of arousal filling my nostrils and setting my body on fire. But this is just the beginning. I intend to push her over the edge and give her more pleasure than she's ever known.

Her breasts are perfect, so perky and sweet. They fill my hands as I brush them over her warm skin. Tugging on her pale pink nipples, I give them a tight squeeze.

"Ahh," she moans and arches against me.

"Is that what you like? A little kinky pinch?" I whisper beside her ear, coaxing her deepest desires to the surface.

She grimaces and shakes her head, but a shudder wracks her as she spreads her thighs, giving me better access to her clit. Her eyes are wide, staring, as she takes in the sights and sounds before her while I play with her beautiful body. Caressing her, making her shiver with need.

Lucas is changing position. Now he's on his side facing us, lifting Casey's thigh so he can ease himself in from behind while cradling her. Her eyes are closed, her mouth open on a gasp. One hand caresses her breast while the other slips over her sex and touches her clit as he moves his hips. Casey cries out as he enters her. She's already so close to orgasm.

As is Astrid.

I nip her neck, enjoying the feel of her pressed against me. She's so wet now, her slit is slippery as I massage my fingers around her mound.

"Do you want him to touch you too?" I prompt. "Make you come alongside her?"

"No," she groans as I speed up the pressure on her nipples and clit. Her breathing is a harsh rasp as she struggles to remain in control.

"Or is it me that you dream about? Making you come so hot and hard. Maybe while they watch?"

"Oh, shit," she says, as her body quivers. "I think he *is* watching us."

Haskell is taking it slow and easy, gazing at us through the ice, clearly enjoying the sight of our kinky sex game. Casey writhes with her eyes closed, lost to the feeling as he thrusts inside her. His arm gently cradles her body, keeping her close and safe while fucking her nearer and nearer to ecstasy.

"He likes what he sees when I fuck you, baby." She's taut like a bow, so close to coming, but I want her to hang on just a bit longer. Build the pleasure until she can no longer resist its pull.

I play with her slit. "You like being stretched by me, don't you baby? You love being filled up inside." Her eyes slide shut as I slip my fingers into the tight sheath.

"Oh, God, Race. I need your cock," she wails, "I need your cock, please!"

I pull her backward, sliding her ass up my chest and over my face, and give her my tongue instead. Holding her steady with my hands on her hips, I lick her pussy. Hot, wet Astrid fills my mouth as I explore her with my tongue and lips.

She cries out and jerks, surprised by the sudden change. But she's swollen and ready. The best thing I've ever tasted. Moaning with need, I thrust my tongue into her core.

She comes in a rush, her body tense as a keening wail escapes her lips. She gushes into my mouth. Her honey-warm taste and sexy cries send me to the edge as her pussy pushes against my face.

I can't hold on as her hand grips my cock. One second of her touch and my balls tighten. Her desire fills me. She wants to see me jizz a hot mess and hear my grunts of pleasure.

I come in a gasp of white hot lightning.

Oh fuck. It's so fucking good as I spurt into the air, her shaky hand pumping me.

"Astrid," I whimper. Her scent and taste fill me. I want to take her again. Make her come even harder. I'm going to get hard fast if she keeps jerking me. And then I'll have her tight little ass that's poised so deliciously above me.

I groan, disappointed as she lets go of my cock and begins to slide off of me. But I let her go. I need to catch my breath so I can bring her to bliss again.

Resting on her side, she smiles at me, her face flushed, her body covered in a thin sheen of sweat. But beneath the pleasure of the rush she's had with coming on my face and making me blow my load like a hot geyser, there's tension I can't understand. Her eyes aren't as full of bliss as I want. And her smile is more tight than real.

"What's wrong?" I ask, my own pleasure fading.

Her smile disappears as she peers through the ice and sees Casey and Lucas, flushed and aroused. They're kissing and fondling, preparing to fuck again, clearly inspired by our sex-capades as Lucas settles Casey's wet pussy over his mouth.

"Oh shit, oh shit," Astrid says looking around for something to cover herself with. "They saw everything, didn't they?"

"It's okay," I insist, using snow from the floor to quickly wipe myself clean. I barely feel the chill as I concentrate on Astrid's sudden anxiety. "They won't remember anything. It will all be just a dream."

"But I will," she says, and the embarrassment is clear in her eyes now. She's shaking from the intensity of it all. "I want my clothes back now, please."

What? Well, damn. We haven't even crested the tip of the fun I have planned. But, even though I'm the one wearing the stupid bracelets, I promised to always give her the choice. And she's looking more uncomfortable than happy right now.

Fuck.

I wave my hand and whisper a command, and we're both fully clothed in an instant. She looks down at herself and traces her hand over her costume in amazement. But her gaze is accusatory as she glances at me.

"Exactly how does this power of yours work? You can do *a lot* more than control the weather."

I shrug lightly, despite the feeling of uneasiness building inside. Did I push her too hard? Give her too much? This isn't how I expected her to react to experiencing the secret desires she has. "I've had a long time to practice. Get to know my limits."

"But you hold yourself back all the time, don't you?"

"I don't want to hurt anyone."

"Don't hold back," she whispers. "Don't hold back with me."

I stare at her dumbfounded. Throughout my entire life, no one has ever asked that of me.

People have either wanted to use me for my power or lock me up because I'm a monster. No one has ever asked me to just be me and accept who I am.

My heart thunders in my veins. I wish I could do what she's asking and give her what she's wants. Every fiber of my being screams to just let go and enjoy what she's offering, but I can't. I need to protect her too.

I shake my head. "You don't know what you're asking."

"You're right. I don't. You keep telling me that choice is important. That I need to trust you. But you need to trust me too. That's been our problem from the start. You didn't trust me enough to even tell me your name. How the hell am I supposed to trust you? How do I know you aren't manipulating me, just like you do to everything else around you? Do you get off on doing this kind of thing? Making people do what you want them to?"

I literally see the suspicion take root.

"That wasn't me," I say. "Everyone in this room is feeding off of what you want them to do."

"Bullshit," she hisses, rising to her feet. "You're just twisting things around again."

"Didn't you ever wonder why Casey is having twins? Think about it, Astrid. On some level it's what you wanted her and Lucas to do."

She stares at me, her mouth gaping and her eyes filled with a mixture of horror and astonishment. She shakes her head. "That's not true."

"Yes, it is."

"It was random chance. I didn't have anything to do with it."

"Maybe," I say to soften the truth. "But you do have that kind of power within you."

"Really? You're so super-powerful. How do I know you're not just manipulating me? Twisting me with your lies?"

I know that, despite the enticing orgy writhing around us and the arousal coming off her in waves, I won't be getting her tight ass tonight or any other night, unless I can come up with something witty and real to say to persuade her otherwise.

But my mind is a dead blank. Because there isn't anything to say to change her mind. The reality is that she has every reason to be suspicious. Can I honestly say that choosing to not manipulate her isn't a constant struggle in my daily life? I shake my head as my heart becomes a dead weight in my chest. This battle was lost before it ever started. "You just have to trust me."

"My point, exactly." She starts to pace, looking for a way through the semi-visible wall. "I have to get out of here."

I could stop her tearing through the thin veil I've cocooned us in, but I promised to always let her choose and that is one promise I will never break, no matter how much panic screams at me to do so.

I follow her instead as she makes her way quickly through the bar, ignoring the maze of naked bodies covering the floor in clusters of twos and threes, and even more.

She doesn't slow once she's outside where the cool night air licks at her pain, trying to numb it. In her blind need to escape, she starts to head for the forest and the dark. But that's where danger lurks, and I can't allow anything to harm her.

"Astrid, wait," I call out. "Let's talk about this. Please?"

She starts to run.

I catch her easily and sweep her into my arms, climbing high into the air as a current catches me.

"Fuck!" she shrieks and clutches at me as the ground falls away beneath our feet. In seconds, I settle us onto the roof of the Ice Hotel.

Her fingers cling tight to my suit. *"Holy shit.* Holy *fucking* shit," she says between gasps as she struggles to catch her breath. "I thought you said you couldn't fly."

"Do you see any wings?" I ask. My Viking cloak billows out behind me as the breeze catches it.

She steadies herself, but doesn't let go as she looks at the drop over the edge into the shadows below. Her eyes are wide, her luminous fear easy to see in the glow from the Aurora lighting the night sky. "Then what the hell was that?"

"The air pushing against gravity and winning. You okay?" I ask her.

She stares at me at a loss for words, her mouth hanging open as if it's the stupidest question in the world.

I take that as a yes and reach up with a finger to gently close her mouth. Placing a quick kiss on her lips, I pull her tight against me, my heart beating fast at the leap I'm about to make. I wanted to wait until morning, to give us this night together at least, but there's no point in waiting any longer. She needs to see with her own eyes why her instincts were right about me. I am a manipulative bastard. The demon of her dreams. Even if it's the last thing I ever wanted to be.

"Are you ready?" I ask.

She licks her lips. The Northern Lights arcing above give her pale skin an effervescent glow. With her full lips and eyes wide, she's more beautiful than I've ever seen, despite the uncertain look in them. "For what?" she whispers.

"To see why you should never trust me."

Before she can blink or breathe a reply, I grip her tightly and push off from the rooftop. The air immediately responds to my control and lifts us high into the night, the sizzle of the Aurora flickering above flooding through my veins like a ribbon of fire, filling me with energy even as my heart dies.

With a crack of thunder vibrating the air, I head toward the center of the forest and my home.

Chapter 8

Ohshit, ohshit, ohshit, ohshit.

I shut my eyes tight and shiver, but it's not from the cold. I swear I can feel the Aurora flowing through me, a tickling sensation that starts in my stomach and spreads outwards through my veins, making me feel more alive than I've ever been.

Or maybe that's just adrenalin and a hefty dose of fear. Because we're flying.

Flying!

I want to scream, yell, freak out, kick Race in the ass.

But every panicked response is whipped away by the icy air stealing my breath. And the knowledge that the only thing keeping me from plummeting to my death is him.

You fucking ass. You fucking, lying ass.

Where the hell is he taking me? His house? The pit from hell he crawled out of?

The world tilts as we change trajectory and my stomach does a little flip. I tighten my hold and bury my face against his neck, keeping my eyes squeezed shut.

"It's okay, baby," he says. His warm breath tickles my ear. "We're almost there."

"Don't call me baby," I hiss between clenched teeth.

God, I hate this. I'm so freakin' freaked and I can't tell what to feel anymore. I want to deck him for every lousy thing he's ever done to me. Make him feel the pain that he's caused with all the lies, the humiliation, the embarrassment with my friends.

But I can't shake the horrible nagging feeling that maybe he's not been lying to me. Maybe I've wanted it all to be lies. It's a hundred thousand times easier than accepting the truth. That the thing that spurred me to race out of the bar, and what I've really been running from all this time is me.

Because being held like this, in his strong arms, with his excited pulse beating beneath his skin, the heat of him, his strength, is both intoxicating and intense. Not to mention his delicious, familiar scent. As much as the desire to hate him throttles through my veins, I can't. He makes me feel safe.

And horny as all fucking hell.

The primal part of me breaks free. The part that doesn't give a shit if all this is some crazy nightmare, and he's a manipulative monster from the deepest bowels of hell. I part my lips and give him a tiny lick, right on his pulsing jugular.

A shudder wracks him. His grip around me tightens and my stomach leaps into my mouth as we suddenly descend.

"We're here," he murmurs.

His cloak slowly settles around us as the wind dies down. Ever so gently, my feet touch the ground. I'm trembling and wobbly, but that doesn't stop the delayed response that should have happened five minutes ago.

As soon as he lets go of me, I slap him.

Hard.

Right across his gorgeous cheek.

"Don't ever do that to me again," I manage between gulps of air. I bend over, placing my hands on my knees to stop the dizzying feeling that the world is falling away. He reaches for me again.

"No," I say and stop him by putting my hand up. "Just give me a moment." Closing my eyes, I steady myself. One breath. Two. Gradually the sickness fades. But my pulse is beating just as fast, threatening to explode my veins with the volatile cocktail of emotions flooding through me. "I hate heights."

I catch his troubled gaze. The pain and regret filling his eyes is easy to see. The anxiety tightening his strong jaw. The darkness around us is fading. I glance toward the source of the light, and my pulse spikes yet again.

The house itself is unremarkable. Typical of what I've come to expect of a traditional Swedish home. Single-story wood frame with rectangular, multi-paned windows. The front door is capped by a porch. A single light glows in a fixture on the wall, giving the entryway a ghostly pall rather than an inviting appearance. Thinking of the dark secrets this place hides, maybe we should have come here during the day after all.

He waves his hand and whispers a word. More lights come on, brightening the rooms inside and pushing back the darkness. The path leading to the porch becomes lit up by tiny globes of light, hidden beneath a crust of snow, showing us the way we need to go.

"Welcome to my home," he says, but there is no joy in his voice. The warmth is gone, replaced by the empty echoes that haunt his eyes.

He holds out his hand for me to take.

I hesitate only slightly. As his long fingers entwine with mine, I can't help wondering if the gesture is meant to steady me or him.

He takes a deep breath. "Shall we go inside?"

I nod. Am I ready to face whatever he's hiding? Not really. But I know it's what I need to do.

The snow crunches beneath my boots as we walk along the path together. His grip is firm as he twists the doorknob. The latch opens without a squeak or any hesitation, allowing us to step over the threshold. I pause on the welcome mat, not wanting to track snow across the polished wood floor.

The inside is surprisingly charming, warm from the lights and the fire crackling in the living room hearth, which he starts with a snap of his fingers. The comforting scent of wood smoke tickles my nose, along with a hint of pine. Everything is clean and tidy. Not what I expected of an empty home. Or one haunted with dark secrets. A covered tray of biscuits has been placed on the coffee table, along with two cups turned upside down on their saucers, waiting to be filled with something hospitable and refreshing.

"Didn't you say no one lives here?"

"I have a housekeeper. She keeps it up for me. And I told her I was coming yesterday, so…" He trails off, frowning as he glances around the place.

"This is where you came?" I say as a few things click into place. "When you got off the plane?"

"Yes," he says. Giving my hand a little squeeze, he lets it go, then strides purposefully across the floor toward the kitchen I can see peeking through an open doorway on the left. "Don't worry about your boots," he says as he disappears from my view. "Make yourself comfortable. I'll get us something to drink. Coffee okay?"

"Yes." Comfortable. Right. In the house of sinful secrets?

But I can't help my curiosity as I take off my gloves and slowly wander around the room. Everything appears just as it should be. The inviting sofa and lounge chairs, slightly worn, but still in good shape. Books are lined up behind a glass-doored cabinet. Hard covered novels of someone's favorites. The Lord of the Rings, volumes 1, 2 and 3 in Swedish. A selection of cookbooks whose titles I can't read.

Knickknacks sit upon shelves, trinkets and memories gathered from a lifetime of experiences that mean nothing to me, but still make me smile. I trace my finger lightly over the horns of a clay reindeer, clearly made by the hands of a small child. Awkwardly beautiful, its uneven eyes stare back at me, its lips pulled wide into a lopsided grin. Race. It must have been made by Race during a happier time. He's never mentioned any brothers or sisters.

Photographs line the walls and rest on the mantle above the fire place, snapshots of a part of his life I've never known. I feel slightly voyeuristic as I study the portraits of people who have shared his life. His wife, smiling and beautiful, before she decided to take her own life. Her presence is strong as I look into her eyes. False happiness. False beauty. Where did it all go wrong?

She haunts him still, I can see that now. Feel it as I purposefully move my attention from her to a set of older portraits hanging on the wall. Sepia toned, this couple looks stiff and formal, dressed in high collars and old-fashioned finery and yet the young woman, at least, is carrying flowers. Her dark hair is tied up in an attractive style, her dark eyes shining bright, despite the lack of a full smile. And the man standing beside her? Holy hell, he could be the spitting image of Race in Victorian times. A blond god, daring anyone not to notice him. I can understand why the woman is smiling inside.

"That's my parents on their wedding day," Race says.

I jump slightly. I've been so focused on the pictures I didn't hear him approach.

He hands me a steaming mug of coffee. It smells divine. Brewed to perfection. Like him. Taking a cautious sip, I glance back at the picture of the couple, and frown. His parents?

"Did they have one of those old-fashioned theme weddings? I thought that was your grandparents." Or maybe great-grandparents.

He shakes his head and takes a small sip of his own steaming mug. With him still dressed like Thor, and his cape draped down his back, the mundane gesture of normalcy seems slightly bizarre. "No. That's my parents. My mother was very pretty, wasn't she?"

I nod absently, while my mind tries to do the math. After a moment I give up and just ask. "How old are you, Race?"

"I'll be eighty-seven next January."

"Whoa." That dizzying feeling of vertigo that seized me when we landed settles on me again. I grasp the mantle to steady myself and glance the length of him. "You look pretty good for an old guy."

He laughs.

"It doesn't take much. Just a stray thought now and then, and a visit here once in a while to recharge. The energy flows through everything. The wind. The trees. The water. But mostly in the Aurora. It burns in my blood like fire when I'm here."

I put my coffee mug down on the mantle and face him more squarely. "That pricking feeling… I thought it was in my mind. That's real?"

"Yes. For people who can sense it. Not everyone can. For most people it's just a light show. For others…something more. The Sami believe the Aurora is a veil of sorts. A thinning between the world of the dead and ours, where spirits come back to visit."

"Is it true?"

His lips pull into a grim line. "I wouldn't recommend going for a walk in the forest on a night like tonight."

I watch him in silence for a moment, unable to think of what to say. Unsure of what to even feel. He's a man beyond my comprehension, who can alter things to suit his will. And clearly he's had a long time to practice. Eighty-seven years old and still gorgeous as if he's barely thirty. He's a man built on lies. I think I can sort of see why perhaps his wife wanted to die, if she loved him, and all he did was lie, lie, lie.

But I don't love him, despite what my own heart has been trying to say since the first moment I saw him and recognized that in some way we were connected. I thought it was desire, but maybe it's more. This god and goddess thing that we share on a level I'm afraid to know. I'm almost relieved if it's the truth. It's better than loving a man who has no soul. Just layers of bottomless lies.

Despite the fire warming my body, I'm feeling cold. "Why did you bring me here, Race?"

"I've made a lot of mistakes in my life," he says. "Unforgivable things I can't undo. And I don't expect that. But you wanted to see who I really am. So here we are."

Taking me by the hand in a grip so firm it almost bites, he pulls me behind him into a hallway off to the right. It separates into three rooms, one big, one smaller and a bathroom at the end. Looking into the larger room, I see a bedroom. It's tasteful, but clearly belongs to Race with the antlers painted on the wall, and the queen-sized bed meant for someone who is tall.

"I inherited this house from my parents," he says. "They left me everything they had. Bruises from my father, from when he used to beat the fuck out of me for being so different. Kindness from my mother, when she tried to stand up for me against him. I taught him a lesson one day. Choked the air from his lungs until he passed out. He left after that. Left us alone to live in a forest. My mother and her little freak son. The kid who couldn't go to regular school because the other children were afraid of lightning."

The bitterness and anger boils off him in waves, but at the heart of it is unbearable loneliness.

Pulling on my hand, he takes me to see the other room. It's a nursery. With a crib and a change table. Stuffed toys lie in wait to be used. But the room is untouched and empty. And I begin to get the sense of where his deepest despair is coming from.

Oh, God.

I start to back out of the room, my heart beating like a drum, but his hold on me is tight and he won't let go. My breathing is fast and uneven. I don't want to be in this room, to see what he's trying to show me. The root of his despair is just like mine.

"Race," I whisper. "Please let me go."

But he's lost in his own tragic maze, too far away from me to hear what I'm trying to say. "I tried, Astrid. Tried so hard to fit in and live a normal life. Tried all my life to master this godforsaken power so I won't hurt people. But, none of it. Not the sacrifice. The long years spent living alone. Nothing I did ever made a difference. In the end I gave up. Decided to take what I wanted instead and not give a shit what happened."

"Race," I try again. His grip on me is almost painful. But that's not the reason tears are stinging the corners of my eyes. Standing in this empty nursery I can feel the hope and dreams that lived here, the happiness he once had. But now it's gone, all gone. A dream empty of promise. Just like the little heart that stopped beating inside me when I was sixteen. The little life that my parents convinced me was a mistake.

The dam inside me breaks and the floodgates open. I'm a hot mess of tears. Ugly gasping tears that soak into his costume as he holds me tight against his chest.

In seconds he has me cradled against him in the living room on the sofa.

"Oh, shit, baby. Shit. I'm sorry."

"I can't—" I manage between gasps. "That room. I can't..."

"It's okay," he whispers, soothing me. "Shhhh." His fingers stroke my hair as he undoes my braids and fans his fingers through the loose strands. Gentle kisses touch my temple, simple touches of devotion I feel all the way to my bruised heart. "You don't have to. You don't have to if you don't want to."

The storm calms a bit after a moment, but the ugly ache is still there. If what he says about me being a goddess is true, I know what I've done. For one brief moment as I stood beneath my parents' disapproving glares, I believed the lie. That the little life growing inside me had no worth. That I was better off without it complicating my life and theirs. And in that moment of doubt I caused my baby to die.

So I can't quite believe that it's true. That my being like him isn't a lie. I don't want to be responsible for the death of my child.

And at the same time, I feel the energy flowing from the Aurora into me, just as it does into him. It makes me want to cling to him, to get beneath his skin, to become everything he's ever wanted and everything I've always feared. We've lived the same life, always on the outside looking in at the happiness, which belongs to others, but could never belong to us. Unless we embrace our truths and stop covering them with lies.

I don't want to love him. I don't want to be like him. And yet, I am.

Tears blur my eyes as I raise my head from his chest and see him looking at me with the same pain that is mine.

He wipes the wetness from my cheek with his thumb and smiles at me softly. "You are so beautiful, Astrid. My goddess. My life."

"Please, don't," I whisper and close my eyes.

He wants to lay himself bare to me. Because I wanted to know. To see him beneath the lies. But I'm not sure I can bear to hear any more truths that are so close to my own. I don't want to see how deep that pain goes inside. "You don't have to tell me any more."

"Yes, I do," he says softly. "You deserve the truth. To see me for who I truly am."

"I get it," I say. "You've lived a fucked-up life. So have I. We've both done some…bad things. You don't need to spell them all out for me."

But he shakes his head. "This one's important," he insists with a rigid smile.

So I wipe the wetness from my eyes with a sweep of my palm on my lashes and wait for my heart to shatter into a million jagged pieces of pain.

"Twelve years ago, I decided to venture into the business scene again. I wanted to make a new start of things. This time do things my way. And if it meant twisting things to get what I wanted? What did it matter? People were destined to get hurt either way." He pauses, his gaze never leaving mine. "That was when I met Charity."

Hearing her name fall from his lips with such bitter loss and regret does nothing good for the misery I already feel, and everything to increase the sickness hitting my stomach like a fist.

"Would she have fallen in love with me anyway? Maybe. She was the perfect candidate for what I wanted. Young, beautiful, innocent, so easy to control. I wanted her to be with me forever. So I made her want that too."

"You made her?"

"Yes."

"I thought you said you could only influence things."

He grimaces slightly and a bitter chuckle escapes his throat. It's a dark, empty sound. "I was very persuasive. I wanted to live a normal life so badly, I didn't give her a choice. I didn't tell her anything about me or show her the things I can do. And for a while, I thought she was happy. Maybe she was. The money, the success in business. Those things seemed to genuinely please her. But after we were married, I started to notice changes. Little things I couldn't fix completely."

"She became distant with me. Withdrawn. I couldn't tell if it was me or the routine of our life. But I was hell bent on finding a solution I could control. I didn't want to let her go."

"You must have loved her very much," I say.

"I wish that were true," he says. "I loved controlling her more, being able to force her to smile, even though it was clear she didn't want to inside."

"A regular Stepford Wife," I say quietly, feeling hot and cold at the same time.

He nods. "I thought having a baby would give her something to look forward to. It was something she had always wanted. Something we had talked about. And when she found out she was carrying my child, the light came back into her eyes."

He doesn't say anything more, just sits there staring into the crackling fire, his heart beating fast. But this, I am certain, isn't the end of his story, any more than it's the end of my own.

"What about you?" I manage to whisper past the lump in my throat.

His gaze stays fixed on the fire for a few seconds longer, before coming back to connect with mine. "I began to worry. What if the baby was different, like me? She was about five months along when I decided to tell her everything about me." The torment is so strong within him, I can feel it bleeding through into the air. It makes me shiver and my fingers tremble as I clutch his strong body tight.

My voice is far from steady as horror sinks into my belly, and I know the answer before I even ask, "Is that when she…?"

"Yes."

Fucking hell. Fucking goddamned shit from hell.

His Adam's apple bobs as he swallows hard. His jaw is so tight I fear it might crack, but his gaze never wavers from mine. Pain is so deep in him, it's a bottomless river that flows into me. Fresh tears prickle my eyes, but these are from anger as much as despair.

"She didn't want to give birth to a monster. Or live her life with one."

"A monster?" The anger starting to simmer inside me becomes a flare of icy rage.

Race is still speaking. I see his mouth moving, but I no longer hear his words as he tries to explain her reasoning. Because I don't give a shit how she did it or why she felt it necessary. Taking her own life is one thing, but to kill her precious, defenseless child in the process is inexcusable to me. And she sure as hell doesn't get to haunt her ex-husband afterwards, making him feel guilty for a choice that ultimately wasn't his.

I cut him off with an impatient wave of my hand. "Where is she?" I glance around the living room, trying to see if I can catch a glimpse of the presence I feel so strongly. I've never been much into the occult or felt a strong connection to the spirit world. Whether it's the Aurora burning through the skylight overhead and into my blood or just the mood I'm in brought on by the painful loss I share with Race, I'm consumed with the need to meet this spirit face to face and end this guilt-ridden charade. "She's still here, isn't she?" I prompt at the surprise sparking through the pain in his gorgeous blue eyes.

"Yes, she…we were on vacation here at the time."

"You should burn this place to the ground," I snap as I push away from him and stand. It's full of so many bad memories for him, I'm surprised it's not a charred wreck by now.

Following my instinct, I head to a door at the back and outside into the night. He shadows me. His hand presses against my shoulder, trying to caution me and hold me back.

"Astrid…" he says, his voice heavy with grief.

The Northern Lights shimmer bright in the night sky, lighting up the snowy ground. The only darkness is the trees, a thick wall of pines standing witness to the garden before me. It's rustic, a tribute to the wilderness it was born from. A massive boulder, easily as tall as Race, dominates one side. Smaller rocks crusted in a sheen of ice have been placed around it amidst berry bushes and barren roses. But it's the monument carved into the trunk of a birch tree that catches my gaze. The sweet little cherub face with chubby cheeks and smiling eyes.

I freeze mid-step onto the hard crust of snow. I've been a fool. It's not the spirit of his wife that haunts him. The one that is pinning him to this place and holding him in its clutches is just a tiny thing. It slips out from behind the tree and hovers there, hesitantly, as if sensing our approach. A puff of breath in the winter air. So insubstantial I can see through it, but I know it's there. If only because of the effect her presence has on Race.

"I tried to stop it. Tried to save her. I wanted her to live so badly, but she was too small." His voice seizes as his grief catches in his throat. And it all makes sense to me now. His pain, his need to keep in control, his desire to hide himself from the world, his aching loneliness. The reason he's kept this house so immaculately in his absence. The heavy responsibility he feels for the spirit of this child he was unable to save but couldn't let go.

Recognizing him, the tiny wisp of mist darts away from the tree to dance excitedly by his face.

His smile is bittersweet and full of tears as he turns to me. "I'd like you to meet my daughter. Her name is Stella."

He speaks of her like she's still alive. Even though this is just a shade, a glimpse of a soul that got left behind. He's been hanging on for ten years, his power influencing her to stay and not pass on, because he can't quite believe that after all his hopes and dreams, she died.

The pain is so great, I'm bleeding inside, but I can't walk away from this.

Not this grief.

Not this man.

And not this lost child.

Tears stream down my face as I fall to my knees. The little wisp darts away as if startled. But then floats closer to me, bobbing hesitantly, curious, almost shy. It brushes against the wetness on my cheek and I feel her question stir like a warm breeze in the sunshine.

Why are you so sad?

I'm sobbing, choked with the grief flowing like a river through me. I miss my son. My sweet baby who I never got the chance to hold. She reminds me of him as I picture him now, a tiny spirit who once fluttered like her. "I'm so sorry, little one," I whisper, my grief encompassing them both. For what has been done. For all the lost time. For what has to happen now.

Can I meet him?

"Yes," I manage to say in reply as the shattered remnants of my heart become bittersweet slivers at the note of curiosity and excitement she has, this lonely little ghost.

She would have been so beautiful. With rosy cheeks and a warm smile. Sun-kissed hair like her father, and cobalt blue eyes.

Race is shaking, kneeling beside me in the snow. His pain is so great it's a palpable thing, turning the sky dark with clouds and hiding the stars. He thinks he's a monster for what he's done. But it's just the love of a father, a lonely desperate man, whose heart beats so strongly inside. I grasp his trembling hand and hold it tight, as tears blind my eyes.

The wisp touches my cheek again. She's so tiny, like a little bird, but so warm and comforting to hold. She whispers another question.

Will you take care of him?

Oh, God. The last shreds of my heart dissolve into a mist of pain. She's been waiting all this time to know that he'll be fine. Hanging on because she loves her father and doesn't want him to be alone.

"Yes," I say. And the decision is suddenly easy to make. As inevitable as the sunrise or the kiss we shared when I first met Race. I've fought the obvious long and hard, so afraid inside to embrace the truth. But now it's the only thing I can feel as my new reality takes root. "Yes," I say more strongly, "I will take care of him."

His sharp intake of breath draws my eyes to him.

Snow is falling, swirling around us and landing lightly in his hair. In the light streaming from the windows, his pain and surprise are clear.

Do I mean it? Yes.

I give him a little smile despite the tears stinging my eyes. There's no way I can ever abandon this man. He's so much like me and I'm like him. The only person I've ever met who filled the lonely places inside. Or understood the pain.

The little wisp darts around, happy and excited, before coming to rest before him.

"Oh, God," he whispers and pulls me into his arms. His hold is tight, so strong and right. He's shaking with the emotion ripping him up inside and flowing into me.

I clutch him close. I don't want to do it, cause him more grief. But I need to set this right. I touch his cheek with my icy fingers. It's wet with the same tears that are shining from my own. The same grief I feel for not protecting my son ten years ago. The same guilt twisting me that I created a life and allowed someone else's choice to take it away.

I may not have been able to change things then, but with the knowledge flickering within me and the Northern Lights burning bright in my blood, I can change things now. I'm a goddess. A child of Sarahkka. And I can send the spirits of children home.

I press on his cheek, turning his face until his eyes lock on mine.

"You have to let her go now, Race."

He flinches as if the words are acid I've tossed in his face. But I don't let go or let him look away. I press tighter into his strong body and keep my palm on his cheek as I gently brush my fingers through his snow-tipped hair.

"You have to let her go," I repeat. "She's ready."

His face is so chiseled with grief it could be cut from ice.

But the little wisp hovers nearby, waiting. A tiny thing filled with sadness and excitement. "It's okay," I whisper. "She won't be alone. My—my son will keep her company—" My throat closes up as my own grief becomes too real to speak.

He moves then, his hands clutching me hard and tight to him. His breath fanning hot against my cheek as he whispers raggedly by my ear, "It hurts."

"I know, baby, I know," I say. I press kisses along his jaw, letting the emotion roiling inside take physical form. He is no monster, despite what he thinks. The special heart he has just needs a safe place to beat. "But you have to let her go now. She needs to be free."

He shudders against me, unable to raise his face from where it rests on my neck. His agony bites into me so strong I want to scream, but I smooth my hands down his back instead, giving him a moment to collect himself as he silently says goodbye.

Slowly, he raises his head.

The soft wisp brushes over his face as if giving him a kiss before darting away again.

"Sweet Stella," he whispers. "I love you too, baby."

With a look of complete desolation etched stark on his face, he raises his hand towards the tree and the little wisp of mist floating by it. His fingers tremble as I entwine mine with his, giving him all the strength I have.

Then together we whisper, "Release."

Chapter 9

The brush of Race's fingers against my cheek feels like the sweetest, most intimate caress, his steady heartbeat calming as it fills my aching soul with its rhythm.

"Tell me about your son," he whispers, his breath soft against my skin.

Naked, we rest entwined together, warm beneath the soft duvet on his bed. I stir against him. We've been silent for so long, cocooned in each other's embrace that his question seems loud, almost jarring. But he fits so perfectly against my body. It's easy to relax and speak of the pain that floats freely in my mind.

"His name was Sean," I murmur against his chest. Saying it out loud is bittersweet, but it feels good to give voice to the heartache. I bury myself further into Race, enjoying the tickle of his hairs against my face and his comforting shower-fresh scent.

As soon as we stumbled our way back inside his house, he undressed us both and took me into the shower. I'm not certain how long we stood there together, holding each other tight, letting the deep soul-wrenching grief wrack through us as the warm water washed our tears down the drain.

Time is a distant thing, belonging to an outside world filled with meaningless expectations and obligations. Enveloped in his strong arms, with his gentle kisses soothing my puffy eyes, and his virile presence easing my sadness, the only reality I need is Race.

I'm exhausted, but I can't sleep. I feel more alive than I have in a very long time.

He places a sweet kiss on my brow and nuzzles his face into my wet hair, as if savoring the scent.

"I was only sixteen," I murmur. "I thought having a baby would fill up the loneliness. Casey always had friends, but I struggled to fit in. So I picked a guy. And got pregnant first try."

It's not something I'm proud of as I think of the surprise I felt. Waking up five days later with my hand on my belly and *knowing*. The excitement that my plan had worked. The fear of what my parents would think. And how over the next few weeks that fear grew and grew and grew inside until I started to bleed. "I didn't know the power I had. Or what it would mean."

"Shhh," he murmurs by my ear, stroking my hair. "You were just a kid."

"It doesn't make it right, though. It was a stupid thing to try. I learned my lesson at the expense of my son's life."

"Did you want him to die?" he asks softly. His hand doesn't falter as it gently caresses my arms, my belly, my side.

I suck in a shuddering breath. "No."

"Then you didn't do it." His eyes hold a deep understanding as the loss he's just experienced becomes something he can define. "As much as we have choice over things, sometimes the gods want to decide."

He's right, of course. About so many things. I didn't want my baby to die. I had doubt. I had fear. But ultimately I cherished his life. It just wasn't the right time.

But I know I'll always remember the little boy who was mine, and who now holds the hand of a little girl as they play together somewhere high above the Aurora in the sky.

Fresh tears prickle my eyes, but he kisses them away, softly, his touch like a butterfly.

"You're so beautiful, Astrid," he says, his voice slightly hoarse with the grief he's shed, but strong with his conviction. "The most beautiful love of my life."

"Oh, God," I say, feeling my heart flicker with a new light as his devotion fills it. The sensation is both frightening and exciting. I'm not certain I deserve his precious gift, but I can't deny how much it means to me to be held by him like this. So close, our hearts beating as one.

A different, more urgent need is building inside. His inviting scent tugs at me. Driving me to grasp the man I need most in the world, and hold him so tight he becomes the air I breathe. Not stopping to examine my feelings, I clutch at him, wrap my fingers in his hair, and bring his mouth to mine.

He settles over me and takes command, as ravenous for my taste as I am for his. He's been quiet after the storm of tears. Seeming unable to discuss his deep grief as he caresses me, while coaxing me to speak of mine. But it burns beneath his surface. Raw. Full of jagged ends. It nips at him, making him edgy as his cock stirs against my thigh.

I moan softly and press into him as the energy between us, the longing, the loneliness, the overwhelming need rises. It trembles though his body as he clutches me. He's lost so much. I want to fill him with all I have to give and replace his pain with pure bliss.

"It's okay, baby," I whisper against his lips. "You don't need to hold back. Let me help you. Use me. I want to feel you fuck me hard."

He shudders against me. His hands grip me almost painfully tight. But I welcome it, welcome it all. Every last ounce of intensity storming through him.

The firm pressure of his lips demands my submission. I part for him without question. His tongue feels divine as it slides inside my mouth. I love it when he takes control. He tastes so good, I'm moaning in seconds. Rubbing my body against him. I want him to erase every shred of agony we've been through. All the loss, pain and despair.

Taking a moment to come up for air, he rolls onto his back and pulls me on top. The gold bracelets he's still wearing catch the light. They cover his arms like a Viking god's. All-powerful and in control. But I also see his vulnerable side as he studies my body and the ravenous need he has to fuck me. His eyes burn with a ferocious light. Primal. Wounded. Fierce.

I shiver with excitement, my pulse rising in reply.

"Turn around," he instructs. "Show me your ass."

I do as he says, and straddling him, I give it a little wiggle.

He rewards me with a light stinging slap and pushes me forward onto my hands. His treatment is a bit rough, but I don't mind. There's so much energy and emotion coursing through us, I just want him to fuck me, hard.

His cock is near my face, erect and ready for me to taste. But I gasp instead, momentarily distracted by the lick he gives me from my clit to my ass.

"Fuck, Astrid." He growls, a low feral sound. "I could eat your pussy forever."

His tongue is like velvet heat as it plays over my swollen lips and dives within my slit, devouring me.

The pleasure is so intense I shudder and almost come all over him.

His fingers press into my hips, holding me in place. "Do you like that, baby?" There's a savage smile in his voice.

I nod, trying to keep breathing.

"Tell me," he insists and gives me another quick lick. "Tell me with your dirty, dirty words."

"Yes," I gasp as the wildness inside of me growls in glee. "I love your fucking, tongue. It's big, like your cock. I want to come all over it."

"And make me swallow your sweet juice?" He licks me, dancing his long tongue over my pussy and into my core.

"*Yes!*" I scream.

Fucking hell, yes. I'm squirming and wet. Dripping with my need to come. He's playing with me, making me wait, but I don't want to anymore.

"Oh, fuck, baby." I moan and push forward farther onto my knees, thrusting my ass in the air, begging him to take me. "Fuck me now. Please."

"Astrid," he says his voice filled with the agonizing heat consuming him. "I need you so badly." His hands grip my ass cheeks as he settles himself behind me. His thighs are strong, his body hard, urging me to use him.

"Fuck me, Race," I plead as desire shakes through me, making my thighs quiver and my tight nipples ache. "Fuck me with your big cock."

I expect his tongue or his fingers, but his tip presses inside my opening. I gasp in surprise. Then a shudder wracks through me, spiralling out from my core at the gorgeous sensation of Race Lindstrom.

"Just a little bit," he says, his voice strained. "Just a little feel." He plunges once. Twice.

It's so dangerous. So fucking dangerous. But I can't resist how good it feels having his thick cock stretching me.

"Oh, God, Race. Oh, oh, oh—" I'm panting. Trying to remain in control. My fingers grip the duvet. Do I want his child? It's too soon to decide. But I know how exciting the idea is with his cock rubbing inside me. The biting hunger to experience all he can give me drowns out the fear I've had. All I want to do is feel him spurting his hot seed and leave the rest in the gods' hands.

His thumb rubs against my clit.

I come in a rush, a keening wail of pleasure that takes me by surprise. It's sharp, almost painful. But I'm spiralling and quivering from the bliss, my core clenching around him.

He sucks in an agonized breath as I gush all over his cock. "*Fuck*. Astrid. You feel too good."

He pulls out quickly and pumps his cock with his hand, releasing hot jizz in a stream. It coats my ass. Slides down between my quivering cheeks.

Breathing hard, he smears it between my crack and over my puckering sphincter. It tingles where it touches me, warm and wet.

"God, I love your come," I gasp. I smear some on my finger and let it tickle my clit. It's enough to put me on the brink again. I buck against him, wanting more.

"Shit," he says. "I'm going to fuck you so hard, baby." He slides his still-hard cock over the sticky wetness on my ass, rubbing it in my crack.

He teases my sphincter with his tip, testing me, but I'm so jazzed I don't care how he takes me. I just want him inside me again. Fast.

"Damn, you're beautiful, Astrid. So sexy." He spreads my ass cheeks.

I feel the pressure as his cock slowly slips in. Just the tip. Then I gasp from the burn as I take his full thickness. It feels so good to have him there that I whimper, almost a sob.

"Astrid?" he asks and starts to slip out. He's still holding back. Concerned for me.

"Oh, fuck, Race," I moan, my voice hoarse with emotion. I reach around and grab his hip, my nails biting into his skin I'm so desperate to keep him inside. "Don't stop, baby. I love your fucking dick in my ass."

As if my words are a catalyst, his inner damn breaks. Like a man possessed, he pounds into me. His thighs rub against mine as he pumps me over and over. Not leaving anything back this time. I moan and buck from the sharp pleasure that fills me with each thrust. So hard his balls slap my clit, as he fucks our pain into oblivion.

"You're so tight," he hisses. "So fucking perfect."

My arms ache from the struggle to take all he has and more. But I'm writhing as much as he is, enjoying the burn and the bliss that consumes me to have him out of control. He's mine. My Viking sex-god. Mine to love. Mine to keep. Full of pain I want to smother. And fill him instead with bliss.

His hand finds my breast. The tip plays against his palm, tight and needy as I bounce and jiggle to his rhythm. The sensation is soft, insubstantial, reminding me of how he touched me with the shower mist. I grit my teeth.

"Pinch it baby," I moan. "Give it a little twist."

But he strokes it lovingly instead. Adoring each curve of my breast.

"Fucking shit, you're beautiful," he says and there's a desperate quality to his voice, haggard, like he's struggling to hold on. "I don't deserve you. I don't. But my God, I can't…" He trails off, his voice filled with agony and frantic need.

"Come with me, baby," I plead. "I want to feel your fire."

His thrusts are short, becoming uneven. His breath is filled with soft, grunting pants. The sound of him so close to orgasm pushes me over the edge as I imagine him filling my ass with his come.

And then he is. Fucking gushing.

His fingers grip my hips tight. "Oh, fuck, Astrid. Oh, *fuck!*" With one last thrust he buries himself deep. His thighs quiver as he empties his hot seed.

"Race!" I scream as the force of his release hits me. It moves like a white hot wave that makes reality shake as it crashes through me with a peal of thunder.

Boom.

The last thing I see is a mist of red before heavenly bliss takes me away on feather light wings to sweet nothingness.

Chapter 10
ASTRID

"How do you do it? Live with the uncertainty?" I ask Lucas. We sit together on a fur-covered pew made of pure ice. Casey stands in the middle of the chapel, speaking with the wedding coordinator. Her red-gold hair is bright in the light from the ice chandelier hanging above, but not as bright as the smile gracing her face.

"Where's Race?" Lucas asks instead of answering me, his gaze never wavering from Casey.

"I don't know," I say not bothering to disguise the anxious tone in my voice. "I haven't seen him all day."

He disappeared somewhere after I passed out from his incredible orgasm. I briefly remember him taking me back to our room at the Ice Hotel and tucking me into bed beside him. I didn't mean to fall asleep without talking things through with him about our future. But I certainly didn't mean to wake up without his warm strong body beside me.

He probably just needs time to be alone and think, just like I do. He took me to his house to show me his dark secrets. But I doubt he expected me to help set him free of them.

Did I do the right thing? Helping him let his daughter's spirit go?

Yes.

I know that in the deepest part of my soul. But what if it's too much grief for Race? What if it's made things impossible between us now? The sex we had last night was amazing, but an undertone clung to the intensity that tasted like goodbye.

The sense of loss I feel about that prospect twists my insides like a sharp dagger. It hurts far greater than it ever should, considering how angry and upset I've been with him over his lies. But I've seen a side of him this weekend that I can't deny, a vulnerable, caring side that's been hidden beneath the layers of half-truths a person like him—and me—needs to put in place to live any kind of normal life and survive.

I'm just like him in so many ways. It feels freeing to have someone with whom I can confide all my insane insecurities. But can I really build a life with him? A life that includes children of our own? How am I supposed to embrace the inevitable pain that loving someone brings once you have to let them go?

"Yo, Luke-ass," I ask him again, and pull him out of the love-struck trance he's in as he watches Casey work her magic and organize their life. "How do you deal with the insecurity?"

He blinks at me. A tiny frown marring his brow. He's a handsome guy, with his dark shaggy hair and the penetrating look in his blue eyes, but he's no Race Lindstrom. And my pulse has never beat triple-time around Lucas, unlike when I'm near my thunder god.

I've embraced Lucas as a friend since the day he walked into Casey's life, but it's always been more like a brother than a lover. At least until last night. That whole experience was as awkwardly complicated as it was erotic, and I'm eternally grateful neither he nor Casey seem to remember any of it. I think. Or is that a different kind of teasing twinkle I can see in his eyes as he studies me?

"What do you mean?" he asks.

I nod toward Casey. "What if something happens?"

"To the wedding?"

"No," I say exasperated. "God, you can be so dense. To her. Or the babies. Or both. How can you handle not knowing for sure if everything will be alright?"

"Oh. I get it." A little grin tips his lips. "You've fallen in love with Race, and now you're all needy and insecure. Right, Ass-turd?" he teases me, using my nickname and enjoying how it always, *always*, makes my left eye twitch.

"No," I say immediately bristling. "Well, maybe a little," I admit at his unconvinced look.

His grin grows wider. "Good. I'm glad." He pats me on the knee in a gesture of affection. "You need someone in your life who can keep your skinny ass in line."

"Oh, my God," I say. "I should never have talked to you about this."

But his fingers tighten on my knee, pinning me before I can scoot away, his expression turning serious. "There are no guarantees, Astrid. You never know for sure. You just have to believe it will all work out. Am I scared shitless? Hell, yeah. What if something happens to Casey? What if I'm not a good dad? We're having twins, for Christ's sake. Who wouldn't be a bit crazy about that?"

I laugh softly, knowing that at least that's one thing I can guarantee will go well for them. And yes, he will be an awesome dad and husband, otherwise I'll kick his ass.

"I love Casey more than anything in the world. She's my rock, my light, my everything. The first thing I see in the morning and the last I see each night. One day it will end, but I'll have lived my life knowing I wouldn't have done it any other way. That's how I deal with the insecurities. I enjoy each second of happiness. And you should too."

His eyes are filled with such warmth, my throat feels thick as I nod.

"But if Lindstrom forgets his place and hurts you ever again, I'll kick his ass. Deal?"

I smile and wipe my eyes. After yesterday, I'm still feeling raw. And that's just my emotions. "Deal."

"What the heck are you two whispering so seriously about over here?" Casey asks, walking toward us. Stopping before our pew, she puts her hands on her hips and studies us. The camera guy trailing in her wake is still recording, so I plaster on my big-fake smile as Lucas says, "Nothing. Astrid's just getting cold feet."

"Really?" Casey says, arching a brow and looking between us. "I thought that was the groom's job."

Lucas laughs and stands. He places a little kiss on her cheek. "Only thing cold in here is the ice, baby. And you're so hot, you're melting it."

I can't help groaning. It's such a cheesy line, but she swoons for him anyway, smiling all lovey-dovey as he wraps his arms about her. She gives a giddy squeal of delight when he picks her up and spins her around in a tight circle, sealing her lips in a searing-hot kiss.

I'd say it's just them playing it up for the camera, except that would be a lie. They are genuinely happy together. And that pang of jealousy I've felt in the past over their relationship turns to impatience as I wonder where the hell Race is. I genuinely miss him being around, searing me with hot kisses. I want to know if he's okay. Last night was a bit more than either of us could handle without feeling burned deep inside.

"We done here for a bit?" Lucas asks Casey with a special smile. "I have something in our room I'd like to give you before I go dog sledding this afternoon."

"Oooh, that sounds fun." Casey's face flushes slightly as she asks, "Is it long and thick and fills me up inside?"

"Hell, yeah," Lucas laughs. "Your favorite lunch…a twelve-inch hero sandwich. You wanna join us, Astrid?"

And this time I'm sure there's something more in his smile as he glances at Casey and they both raise their eyebrows at me. Damn Race and his *"last night will all be just a dream"* theory. I'm sure they remember seeing *something*, even if they haven't yet said.

I shake my head. I have no interest in being a third wheel in some decadent food-play thing or whatever they have in mind. The whole idea would fall flat for me without Race there anyway.

"I think I'll go for a walk instead," I say. Maybe he's gone back to his house in the forest to grieve privately. Maybe he's out walking, waiting for me to join him for another snowball fight. Or maybe he's decided to ditch me now that I've shredded the ghosts from his past.

The sound of the heavy chapel door opening turns all our heads. A gust of cold air from outside brings with it a swirl of fresh snowflakes that float around Race as he enters the room. My pulse instantly accelerates at the way he walks down the aisle between the columns of ice and rows of pews. He's all gorgeous confidence, filling the room with his presence. And I'm wondering how anyone could ever mistake him for an ordinary guy.

His dark winter clothing is a sharp contrast to the white chapel as the light of the many ice-embedded candles plays over his strong body. There is no uncertainty in his stride as he walks toward me, but the look on his face is tight instead of bearing a smile.

I hear someone gasp, and realize it's me. I've risen from my seat without knowing and now stand beside my pew, waiting for the axe to fall. Something must be wrong for him to look this uptight. And he's not wearing the bracelets anymore.

He glances around the room, taking in the others, and comes to a halt. "I need to speak with Astrid alone."

Chapter 11
RACE

"Yeah, sure," Haskell says and tugs on Casey's hand, jarring her out of the stupor she's in as she studies me. She seems reluctant to leave as she glances at Astrid, concern for her friend crossing her face.

"Come on," Haskell says giving her a little push to get her moving toward the door. "Let's give them some space. It'll be fine."

"But—what?" she looks at Astrid again. "You okay?"

Astrid nods, her smile tight rather than reassuring.

Haskell raises his brow at me, and I nod in reply.

He smiles, looking pleased, and maybe he understands the leap I'm about to take. He's been here before me and knows what's at stake. He murmurs something reassuring to Casey as he scoots her through the doorway and into the snow swirling outside. The camera crew and wedding planner follow closely behind, sharing curious glances.

The silence in the chapel seems to thicken with the sound of the door closing behind them and giving us some time alone.

It's beautiful. The columns of ice shimmering with light. The slanted ceiling and its ice chandelier, giving off an ethereal glow. The perfect setting for what I'm about to do.

But as I stand here looking at Astrid's pale, worried face, I wonder if I haven't made yet another mistake. It's too soon. I've been down this path before. Except there are no guarantees of the answer this time. I want her to say yes with all of my soul, but that choice is up to her to decide.

The idea should have me anxious, but instead it's freeing. The lack of control is almost invigorating. I'm lighter than I have ever been in my life. My love for her will be the same, no matter what she chooses to do.

My guilt over Stella is still as sharp, as agonizing as the day ten years ago when I tried to save her from Charity. But it's different now, less deep, bandaged by the connection I share with the woman standing before me.

My goddess. My love.

She knows the darkness I live in and what I've done.

The monster that I am.

She's seen me cry.

But she hasn't run away like I feared. Instead, she helped release me from the pain I've been keeping inside for longer than I can remember. Her incredible, beautiful soul is the light of my life, making the world a place I can exist in. And I don't know what I'll do if she chooses to say goodbye now. But it's a risk I'm willing to take in order to make her happy.

"Is everything okay?" she asks, her voice full of hesitation.

"Yes," I say. "At least I hope so. It depends on what you think."

"About what?" Her voice is barely above a whisper but I can hear it so clearly in this silent room. The light plays softly against her skin, lighting up her beautiful eyes and gorgeous, kissable lips. But I can't indulge in the need burning inside me to taste her. Not yet. And if this all goes to hell, maybe never again.

I bend down on my knees onto the snowy floor before her. Her eyes grow wide as I reach into my pocket for the small box burning a hole inside it.

"Oh, my God," she whispers and covers her mouth with her hand as I pull the package out and hold it for her to take. She hasn't accepted any of my gifts so far. And I'm not certain if this will go any different. Seconds pass while she stares at the white box resting on my open palm, her mind churning, trying to decide if what she suspects inside it is something she really wants.

I want to pop it open and show her, make the decision for her, but choice is so very important between us.

So I wait, watching every flicker of her lashes and the way her tongue darts out to wet her lips as her breath passes between them, accelerated and alive.

The anticipation is killing me. So badly, I want to know what's on her mind, to grab her tight and kiss her hard. I almost groan when she reaches forward with tentative fingers and picks up the box.

Cracking it open, her eyes grow even wider. Her gaze darts to mine.

I nod, answering the silent question burning in her eyes.

Her beautiful gaze mists with tears as she stares at me then back at the ring, her hand whipping up to cover her mouth again.

"You didn't like the bracelets," I explain. "I thought this might be more your size."

I can't stand it anymore. Rising to my feet again, I grasp the thin band of gold from the ring box and hold it up for her to see. The diamond glitters in the chapel light, sparkling with a brilliance matched only by her glistening eyes.

"Oh shit," she whispers as she takes her hand from her mouth and sucks in a shuddering breath.

"I was thinking something more along the lines of, 'Thank you, Race. It's beautiful,'" I say and the uncertainty inside me shifts a little as a giggle passes her lips.

She takes the ring from me, her fingers shaking slightly as she turns it around examining it as if amazed by its simplistic design. "It *is* beautiful," she says.

"I'm not expecting an answer now," I explain. "I know it's too soon for you. But I know I will never find another woman as special as you. I've waited so long to find you, Astrid. I lost hope along the way. But ever since I saw you at that convention in Chicago, I've known. And after last night…" I pause, unable to put into words exactly how what she's done has affected me. "I want to give you something to show my commitment to you."

"Commitment," she murmurs, her lips turning down at the corners just slightly, as if the word is distasteful. "You want to tie me to you forever?"

Considering the events of last night, her words bite deep. I can't blame her for wanting to be sure of the meaning behind my gift. If anything, it's the other way around and I'm tying myself to her. But whether she accepts the ring or not, my commitment is just the same.

"I love you, Astrid. I want to share my life with you. Not hold you hostage."

"I see," she says, nodding.

"You see?" I repeat, my stomach clenching. I've bungled this somehow. I've never been good with words. I'd rather show her how much she means to me by fucking her senseless again. "That's it?" I ask as my heart squeezes tight.

"Well, I'm not sure." Her eyes flash at me, her teasing look making her serious tone a lie. "Usually a ring like this comes with a very specific question. But I haven't heard it yet."

Pulse thundering in my veins, I get back down on my knees and grasp her hand in mine. I keep my eyes locked on her teary ones. I want her to see the truth burning in my soul. "Astrid Bitten. My goddess, my love. Keeper of my heart. Will you marry me?"

Her whole being lights up, shining in her eyes and her smile. And I know I'll keep this moment inside me forever as she falls to her knees and wraps her trembling body around mine. Her hot breath tickles my cheek as she gives me a quick kiss and whispers the answer I've been waiting for since the moment we met.

"Yes."

***

"It's so pretty," she murmurs beside my ear as she lazily holds her hand up to the light, enjoying the sparkle of her ring in the effervescent glow of the Northern Lights filling our room.

I tuck her closer beside me in the bed. "I used some of the gold from the bracelets to make it, but had to go into town for the diamond," I explain, tracing my fingers over the slender contours of her hand. The ring is a perfect fit, but pales in comparison to her beauty.

"Is that where you were this morning?"

I nod.

"I missed you," she murmurs and her soft lips brush mine in a too-short kiss full of hunger. I chase her mouth, pressing her back against the pillow. She's impatient beneath me, but I take my time showing her how much I've missed her too, with strokes of my tongue against hers, and little nibbles on her full lips. I love the way she tastes slightly minty and like hot, wet desire.

I want to savor every moment. Every lick, every shudder, every little moan of pleasure. She's my goddess. My bride. I can't be this lucky, but I am. After all the long years of my life, I've found someone to share it with. The only person in the world who's ever truly chosen me. My heart is filled with so much love over what she's done, it aches. A beautiful new pain I willingly embrace.

The fact that we can look forward to this for the rest of our lives is like heroin in my blood, urging me on with the need aching inside to fuck her hard, then soft, then hard again until we both pass out from the bliss.

She moans, moving restlessly against me as I wrap her slender wrists in my hand. Stretching her arms above her head, I pin her to the bed.

"You like that, don't you baby? You like it when I take control."

"Yes."

"What else do you like?"

She squirms beneath my gaze and that delicious blush I crave flushes the skin between her breasts. "You," she says looking me straight in the eye, her voice full of husky need. "Just you. Filling me up inside." She bites her bottom lip as her gaze slips down my chest, seeking my hard cock where it juts between us, pressing between her thighs.

I move off of her slightly, to give her the view she craves. "You want this?" I tease. As I stroke my taut skin, the tip of my cock brushes her leg, leaving behind a wet streak of pre-cum.

"Oh, God yes," she groans, barely able to contain her excitement. "Don't hold back for me, baby. I want to feel you coming inside my pussy this time."

My cock twitches in my hand at her pleading tone and the intense desire burning in her eyes. I want to slide into her slick pussy so badly that I can barely breathe. My entire being quakes to be with her like that, to let go and experience the overwhelming bliss. Last night was a taste I could barely resist. But it's not a decision to be made lightly or in the heat of arousal. The loss of my daughter is still strong within me and I know it's the same for her over her son.

"Are you sure that's what you want? We can enjoy each other in other ways just as much." So many ways that we haven't even tried yet.

She shakes her head. "I took your ring. I chose you. All of you. Every last ounce that you have to give me. And in return I give you all of me. There are no secrets. Nothing left to hide." Her beautiful eyes shine as she puts on a wavering smile. "And if that means we're blessed enough to create a new life, then that can only be a good thing, right?"

A tear escapes her hold and trickles down her cheek. "Oh shit, baby. Oh shit." I let go of her wrists and my cock and hold her tight to me instead, concentrating on kissing away her tears. Except I'm pretty sure some of the wetness on her cheeks is from my own. "You are so beautiful. So incredible. So…hot," I say as her fingers snake between us and wrap around my cock.

She gives it a little tug.

Stars explode before my eyes as she spreads her legs wider and guides me to her slick heat. Her wet pussy envelops my tip. I grit my teeth from the effort of not giving in to my most primal need to plunge inside her in one swift thrust and fill her with my seed.

"You're absolutely sure?" I ask again. I need to be certain. I don't want any lingering questions to ever haunt me again. And I know what it will mean for her to carry my child. "I'll get you pregnant if we want it to happen." There is no 'if' about it. It's a certainty for us. It's what we both desire deep down inside. But are we ready?

She cocks her head, a smile brightening her blue eyes. "Why don't we leave that up to chance to decide," she says and lifts her legs, wrapping them around me, and pushing me farther inside.

I lift my head to look into her eyes. She's full of desire, and happiness, and something so powerful I'm almost afraid to breathe.

"I love you, Race," she says, and that beautiful, beautiful soul I glimpsed the first night we shared, seeming a lifetime ago, soars free, lighting her eyes and smile.

"Astrid…" is all I can manage as my heart stutters and starts again with the gift she's given me in her body and words. "Ah, my love. My sweet, sweet love."

I can't hold back anymore. I thrust my hips. My cock plunges deep inside her tight heat.

A shudder takes her, her pupils growing wide and unfocussed from the pleasure rippling through her core and gripping me.

We both moan from the exquisiteness of being with each other like this. Unguarded. Unafraid of the love we share. It burns so deep. An eternity.

She holds me tight. My body and soul. There are no lingering fears.

"The choice will always be yours, my goddess," I whisper by her ear.

And wrapped in her love, I give myself to the ancient, primal rhythm that promises to consume us in a lifetime of utter bliss.

The End

About the Author

Felicity Kates is a mild-mannered manager by day. At night, she trades in her high heels for bunny slippers and lets her imagination run wild. Felicity enjoys writing bold, sexy stories that combine humor with strong characters who know what they want and aren't afraid to go get it. Every story is an emotional journey where the characters must struggle to find their happily ever after. But they do always reach it together in the end, no matter the time or place in the universe.

Felicity lives off of coffee and dreams and enjoys going for walks along the shores of Lake Ontario, taking pictures of whatever catches her eye. A romantic at heart, she loves to snuggle under a blanket with a good book to warm up the cold Canadian winters. When not writing, can most often be found enjoying the quiet company of her husband and son, whom she loves very, very much.

Dear Reader...

Thank you for reading My Destiny. *I hope you enjoyed Astrid and Race's journey to find their happy ever after. I love to hear from my readers, so please drop by and leave me a review at the vendor of your choice. You can also email me directly at felicitykates.author@gmail.com*

For up to date information on my books, including upcoming releases and giveaways, please sign up for my newsletter *http://madmimi.com/signups/123923/join and join my* Kate's Korner Facebook Fan Group *https://www.facebook.com/groups/KatesKorner/*

You can also find me at:

My Website http://www.felicitykatesauthor.com/

Goodreads https://www.goodreads.com/author/show/8345046.Felicity_Kates

Twitter @Fun_Felicity

Facebook https://www.facebook.com/FelicityKatesFun/

Pinterest https://www.pinterest.com/KateReedwood/

Also by Felicity Kates

My Desire (Steam Bunny)

My Decadence (Super-Sex Me)

The Little Miss Kick-Ass Collection (Undressed)

Project Hell – Part One

Project Hell – Part Two

Coming soon…Project Hell – Part Three, Four and Five

More Paranormal/Fantasy Romance You Will Love

THE SCRIBBLER GUARDIAN: ARKS OF OCTAVA
BY BESTSELLING AUTHOR LUCIAN BANE

Jeramiah Poe isn't just any character in the Realm of Fiction; he is Muse Master—Destiny Diviner—Mysterious Miskriat. Being of neither the Traditional Genre Provinces nor Independent, Poe enjoys an eternal lease on life, so long as his Scribbler keeps him out of publication.

Poe meets Kane, a seven-year-old boy from the Independent Horror Province, where he learns ancient codes are being broken and the horror that should be an act, is real. But the evil clutching Octava is not new and Seven Arks have been sent to Earth to stop it. Only something has gone wrong and Poe is commissioned as the 8th Ark of Octava to discover what has become of the Seven. But his passage to Earth comes with revelations he's not prepared for. Not only does his Scribbler not know of his existence, he's a she that his human form seems allergic to. Poe soon realizes that with each Ark he locates, his powers grow along with his feelings for the Scribbler. And the enemy will try and use both to gain control of the two realms.

Available at Amazon.
For more information about Lucian Bane and his work, please visit his website at: http://lucianbane.com

Made in the USA
Charleston, SC
15 March 2016